EXTRA CLASS

The First Crush

GRAPEVINE INDIA

Published by

GRAPEVINE INDIA PUBLISHERS PVT LTD

www.grapevineindia.com

Delhi | Mumbai

email: grapevineindiapublishers@gmail.com

Ordering Information:

Quantity sales: Special discounts are available on quantity purchases by corporations, associations, and others. For details, reach out to the publisher.

First published by Grapevine India 2024

Written by Sachin Garg

Printed at Nutech Print Services - India

To,

First crushes

1

'Welcome to the beginning of a never-ending rat race,' said my best friend Saransh, the master of crude and juvenile humour. He was holding out a brown plastic rat in his palm as I walked towards him at the main gate of Pragati Vidyalaya.

'Don't tell me you're going to take that stupid little thing to class,' I said.

'Why not? It's an opening day gesture. Imagine hundreds of years from now, whenever our classmates look back at their first day of class 11, what will they remember?'

'Hundreds of years from now, all our classmates will be dead.'

'They won't remember what our teachers said. They won't remember how many marks they got in class 10. But they will definitely remember that some guy had brought a rat to their school in Faridabad and caused drama.'

I was in no mood to entertain his absurdity. So I gave him a blank look and continued marching towards the classroom of 11th A. It was our first day at school after the board exams and all everyone wanted was to take it easy for the year before 12th. Except me, of course. I had other plans.

Saransh continued spewing randomness, 'I am going to throw this at our new class teacher and spoil his first lecture!'

'Just grow up, *bhai*,' I said. In the last five years, the only thing that had remained constant was his childishness.

'That's the whole point. I don't want to grow up so soon. The rat symbolises the cutthroat race that's ahead of us and I want to throw it away. Gone are the days of colourful projects and visits to the zoo. 11th and 12th standards are going to be only about scores and extra classes and goals and future plans and whatnot. It's net practice before the actual match and I am not ready yet,' he rambled on.

'Why am I friends with you,' I said, more to myself than him.

'What will you get by being so serious? I think the best solution is that you should just get a girlfriend. Only a nice *bhabhi* can solve all these issues you have.'

'Can I pay you to be quiet.'

'What's wrong with what I said?'

'I don't have time for any girlfriend or anything. I have to focus on my goal. And the last thing I need is a distraction in the form of a girlfriend.'

We entered the school building and all the talk about girlfriends went out of the window, thankfully. Saransh murmured, 'You sure? The girls seem to have gotten much hotter this year.'

Funny and rebellious with a slightly inappropriate sense of humour, Saransh had been my close buddy ever since he joined Pragati Vidyalaya. From 7th standard to now, a lot had changed, apart from his height. While I had grown into a decent 5.11 frame, Saransh was still 5 feet 6 inches tall. Puberty had been great to me and my jawline. But it didn't give much to Saransh apart from a few pimples. He still had a chocolate boy face and an annoying yet likeable personality.

But I guess his appearance affected him more than he let on. So, he found a coping mechanism in being witty and sarcastic instead. I knew that, which is why I always played along when he passed snarky remarks about others.

We finally reached our new classroom. Class 11. Exactly the same as the last room, apart from the benches being bigger by just a few centimetres. The section column didn't read a letter of the alphabet any more. It read 'Science'.

'Have you noticed how everyone is trying so hard today,' Saransh said, as we walked in. We plonked ourselves on the last bench as he continued checking everyone out. He looked like that reality show judge who is way too hard to impress. 'There's Mehul. There is at least half a bottle of gel in his hair today. I bet PT sir will tell him to go to the washroom and wash it all off.' I didn't participate much in the conversation, but didn't mind listening to him. That's how we mostly were. Saransh was the gabber and I was the listener.

As different students entered the class one by one, Saransh continued to make up stories about them. 'Chaitanya dedicated his entire summer to watching European football leagues and thinks he is finally cool.' 'Ananya's favourite thing to consume is a steady dose of Netflix shows.' 'At least 30% of the boys made an attempt at learning to play the guitar this summer.'

Having had enough of this, I decided to pause his non-stop commentary and asked him, 'So, what's the deal with our new teacher? Why do you already hate him?'

'Oh, Mr Gajendra Mishra? He is a full-on wannabe. He thinks he is Raj Aryan from Mohabbatein but in reality, he is just a people pleaser. I've heard he has already sent follow requests to a lot of our classmates on Instagram.'

'That's kinda shady. He couldn't even wait till the first day of class? But please don't throw that rat at him.' Saransh gave a silent smirk, but having known him for so many years, I heaved a sigh of relief, realizing that he had given up on the idea.

My focus shifted to the classroom's entrance, as I saw two new joinees enter, a guy and a girl.

It was reason enough for Saransh to

start gabbing again. 'This guy is a great representation of the Oxford Dictionary Definition of a teacher's pet,' he said. The boy was wearing a uniform as white as they show in those detergent commercials. His round-rimmed thick glasses and shiny shoes definitely aligned with my friend's assessment. The new guy was a little chubby and wore a tie knotted so perfectly that he might have used a ruler to measure its proportions. His hair was short, the kind which doesn't need combing and it came straight on his forehead. The aloof expression on his face suggested that he was convinced that he was superior to everyone.

'He is the kind of guy who would remind the teacher of the homework, in case they forget to check it,' Saransh said.

While the guy came across as a bit too confident, the girl scanned the entire classroom rather nervously. She was petite and looked somewhat fragile. 'And the girl's favourite singer is Taylor Swift,' Saransh said. Somehow, that was also quite believable. I smiled. She was pretty, with a fair complexion and light brown eyes. Her hair was tied back but not braided. Little marks on her cheek told a story of acne, which had now somewhat receded.

'Even though her uniform is as impeccable as her male friend,' Saransh said, 'it comes from a different place.'

'What does that mean? You mean it comes from a different shop?'

'While the guy wants to stand out, hers is more to fit in. It's as if she is seeking the room's approval on whether she can enter.'

'Says the neediest guy I know.' Something about the girl made me want to defend her.

Then an extra enthusiastic 'Good morning' rang in my ears and startled me. Our class teacher had entered the room. I waited for Saransh's educated comments. I was beginning to enjoy them as his observation for most people seemed to be on point. He finally said about the teacher, 'This guy thinks he can be a friend to the students, but he will only end up making a fool of himself in trying to be so.'

The teacher smiled silently, with a bag under his armpit. The moment he kept it on the table, he remembered that he had forgotten the attendance register in the staff room.

'Sir, should I go and get the register?' the new boy said, even before Gajendra Mishra could say anything.

'This newbie is a DCP,' Saransh whispered.

'What's that?' I asked.

'DCP means 'Desperate Class Participation'. Students in this category could go to any lengths to make a good impression.

Meanwhile, the teacher picked a chalk stick and wrote in bold letters on the board, 'MR. GAJENDRA MISHRA.'

After a dramatic pause, he said, 'Hello friends. That's right, friends, not students.' For the first 20 minutes or more, Mr. Mishra went on and on about his philosophy as a teacher. He also shared how he tried hard to make Physics fun for everyone. With every out-of-syllabus sentence he blurted out, Saransh's statements about him seemed more and more precise.

Once his rehearsed speech was over, he started talking more about himself. The more the teacher talked, the darker Saransh's comments about him became. 'This guy is the embodiment of all things incompetent,' Saransh whispered. 'Given his regressive outlook and below-average IQ, he should not have been allowed anywhere within a kilometre of any impressionable mind. But instead, our school, Pragati Vidyalaya, has found him suitable to teach Physics to classes 11 and 12.'

I wanted to remind Saransh of the acute shortage of Physics teachers in the area, but I refrained. The teacher asked everyone to introduce themselves, adding what they wished to do after finishing school. This made for perfect fodder for Saransh to make fun of everyone. I tuned out his blabber and tried to focus on my classmates' introductions. The first 7 people wanted to be engineers. There were 3 aspiring doctors after that.

The new admissions sitting in front of us went before us. The boy said something about wanting to be the best in the world in whatever he did. I didn't pay much attention as I was curious about the girl's introduction. When her turn came, she stood up but said nothing for a couple of moments. Her body language was rigid and tense. Then she took a deep breath and closed her eyes. 'My na-name is Radhika,' she stammered. 'This is my first day at Pragati Vidyalaya and I want to be an AI-ML engineer.' She sat quickly, seemingly relieved at having finished the task of speaking publicly.

When Saransh introduced himself, he said he wanted to be a house husband. The entire class laughed and he pretended to take offence at their inconsideration.

And then it was my turn. 'My name is Yogesh Mittal and I will be an entrepreneur,' I said.

'Will be?' I heard an immediate reaction from the seat right in front of me. It was the guy among the new joinee duo. The question could have been innocent, but the tone came across as mocking. To quash my doubts about his motive behind the question, he added, 'What are you going to start, a *chai* shop?'

Saransh was opening his mouth to say something, but I squeezed his arm, signalling him not to. But I couldn't help my eyes wandering towards the new joinees. I caught a glimpse of what looked like a light slap that the girl did on the boy's wrist. My eyes met hers for the first time and we exchanged a faint smile. Somehow, the feeling of agitation in my heart was immediately replaced by a pleasant warmth.

'You shouldn't have let that go,' Saransh said as soon as I sat down.

I nodded at him, as if nothing needed to be said. It wasn't the first time we were having this chat. When Saransh and I were new friends in class 7, someone had called me '*Chapraasi*'. A few months later, the word '*Jhuggiwala*' was used for me. Instead of fighting or answering back, I froze. In my head, the insults weren't completely inaccurate. The thing was that my family could afford to send me to Pragati (which wasn't even an expensive school) only through the reservation for students from an economically weaker background. The problem was that not only was I from a poor family, but I also looked like it.

While I just stared in shock at those comments, Saransh went and punched each and every one of them. But at some point, the words stopped pinching. I realised they were meaningless and my energies were better used in following my dreams rather than trying to shut everyone down. I began to feed off them instead. In my head, I was convinced that in a few years, most of these guys would be sending me their resumes, looking for jobs in my startup.

I just went about my day, trying to zone out from whatever Saransh was saying. Instead, I attempted to make sense of the incomprehensible stuff my teachers were ejecting on us. By recess, I was a little drained and wanted to get done with the classes already. Saransh wanted to stand in front of the class and mimic the teachers who had taught since the morning. Mimicry was his favourite thing to do.

As Saransh began to gather an audience in the recess, I noticed the new girl smiling right at me. It was hard not to smile back at her. I had a feeling she wanted to say something to me, but her social awkwardness was holding her back. She joined Saransh's audience, but she was the only one looking at me instead.

2

I am usually not the first one to strike up conversations with newcomers at school. However, there was something about her that made me want to speak to her. So, I walked towards her and signalled her to move a little away from Saransh's commotion.

'Hi,' I finally said.

'Hey, I just wanted to apologise on my friend's behalf. He is an idiot and has no filter.'

'It's alright. I know if I walk on this unconventional path, blocking small-minded folks is the first thing I will have to do.'

'That's quite a positive way to look at it. I'm Radhika, by the way.'

'I'm Yogesh,' I said and wondered if we should shake hands. But we didn't. 'You haven't brought lunch?'

'No, I couldn't. Do you have a canteen here?'

The next thing I knew was that both of us were walking towards the ground. As I left the classroom, I glanced at Saransh, who had that look on his face. On the surface, he was mocking the tongue movement of the Math teacher as she spoke, but his eyes followed my exit from the classroom very closely. We might be 16-year-olds already, but Saransh was going to pull my leg for talking to a girl like we were 9.

Once Radhika had taken her egg roll from the canteen, the two of us decided to walk around the ground. Just a day earlier, I couldn't have imagined strolling around in Faridabad's April heat. But somehow, being in school, it seemed completely normal to do so. The scene was chaotic on the ground. One group of class 5 boys was playing football with a cricket ball. A mixed-gender group was playing Dog and the Bone. I noticed that Saransh had followed me to the ground. But to be fair to him, it was probably because he coached a group of class 7 boys in the beautiful game of *marampitti* during his recesses for the last 3 years.

'It's just that Jigyaasu thinks –' she said.

'Jigyaasu?'

'My friend, who was sitting next to me.'

'His parents named him Jigyaasu? Poor guy,' I said.

She chuckled. 'He is on a mission that he has assigned to himself. He wants to be the Head Boy of this school. He is going to do everything he can to impress every teacher here.'

'Tell him I wished him the worst of luck.'

'He is not a bad guy,' she said. 'He said that about you only because he thinks boys just say they will be entrepreneurs to sound cool. And never actually do anything.'

'He is not completely wrong.'

'Yeah, I mean, would you start your first start-up immediately after college or do you want to work for some years?'

'Entrepreneurs don't wait,' I said.

'You mean you'll start immediately after college?'

'Sooner.'

'Alongside college?' she asked.

'Earlier.'

'Immediately after school?'

I just smiled.

'You're going to start now?' she prodded.

'Earlier than that.'

'What is earlier than now?'

'Three years ago,' I told her.

'You started your business three years ago?'

I nodded.

'When you were in class 9?'

'Class 8.'

'Are you serious?' She seemed a little shocked.

I smiled again. I had nothing to prove to anyone. If she didn't want to believe me, I was not going to convince her.

'So, what kind of business is it?' she asked.

I'm usually a subdued guy. People tell me they rarely hear any modulation in my voice. But the moment it comes to my babies, my ventures, I'm a different person. 'Have you noticed how we have to carry the same books to school every day, even though we never use many of them at home?'

She nodded.

'Haven't you wished you had a locker in school where you could just keep them, instead of lugging them home everyday?'

'Oh, yes. Definitely. I once read an article, which talked about how India had the heaviest school bags and the negative impact it has on students' physical and mental health,' she said.

'Exactly. Now, imagine there was an option of keeping your books in a locker in school, just the way they show in American teen movies. Wouldn't you happily pay 200 rupees per month for that?'

Radhika thought about it for a second and then nodded enthusiastically. 'But where did you get these cupboards?'

'I had a partner. Veepi *bhaiya* was in charge of some empty rooms which were going to be the future Physics Lab,' I told her.

'Veepi *bhaiya* was some senior?'

'No, no. He works as an assistant in the Physics Lab.'

Radhika smiled. Seeing her smile made me realise that Jigyaasu's caustic comment was not really a bad thing to have happened. It was only thanks to him that we were having this conversation. I realised that despite being 16 years old now, I didn't have any sensible or mature friends. Hanging out with Saransh made me think that friends just goof off. I didn't know this feeling of actually opening up to someone who was genuinely a good listener.

'It was called BookMyTijori.com,' I said.

Radhika laughed so loudly that some people around us turned their heads. 'You mean like BookMyShow?'

I sensed a hint of mockery in her tone, but I nodded again. In the next few minutes, I told Radhika everything that came to my mind about my first business. I told her about how I sold out all the lockers within a week of starting. The hall with all the almirahs was more packed than a metro at Rajiv Chowk at peak hour.

'But wait a minute,' she said. 'How did the teachers react to this?'

'Well, contrary to what I was expecting,

they didn't make me shut it. I believe the principal saw the possibility of some media coverage through this.'

'But I have a question,' she said.

I was enjoying the curiosity. It was not everyday that I discussed my work with someone.

'Why not just keep a register and make people mark their entries with a pen? Would be so much simpler, especially in a school like ours which doesn't allow students to carry phones.'

I smiled. I had heard this before. 'You're missing the bigger picture. Pragati Vidyalaya was just the beginning. The idea was to go to tens and hundreds of schools. To expand beyond Faridabad, into every city where students don't like carrying their bags.'

'Which is pretty much every city in India.'

'Wrong.'

'What do you mean?'

'Every city in the world,' I said.

'You're so right. Then how is BMT doing now?'

'Well, after it became a success at our school, I was in talks with the nearest Kendriya Vidyalaya for a BMT installation on their premises. And you know, KVs are government schools spread across the entire country. We could've gone big!'

'So, then what happened?'

'Umm, so, six months into the business, an oversmart guy brought an iPhone to school and kept it in his locker. And the idiot had harped to the entire class about how his Dubai *wale taau ji* had gifted it to him. He was going to show it to everyone during recess.'

'Oh, no,' she said. She already had an idea where the story was going.

'It not only got stolen. It got stolen on the very day when the officials from Kendriya Vidyalaya had come to our school to inspect the workings of BMT. Veepi *bhaiya* was given a one-month unpaid suspension and I was made to shut everything down,' I shared with a heavy heart.

I had hoped it would stop hurting so much, but it didn't. My million-dollar business idea came down crashing in a matter of hours. My dream of taking it to other cities remained incomplete. 'Maybe Jigyaasu is right. Maybe, I don't have what it takes,' I said.

'What are you saying? You did much more than anyone can ever dream of. You have a long life ahead of you. It's okay. You will get there!'

Hearing her say that definitely made me feel better. She didn't have to say those things, but I could see that she meant it. I wished the conversation could go on forever as it felt quite refreshing to share these things with someone. But the bell rang and the recess was over.

It struck me that we had only been talking about me but I wanted to know about her. I had so much to ask her. I was eager to find out why she was so nervous while introducing herself to the class. She seemed so much at ease during our walk. She didn't stammer even once when we spoke.

As we walked alongside, I couldn't wait to find out where this friendship would go. I wanted to know everything about her. What excited her? What made her eyes twinkle? Who did she look up to? And more. But we hurriedly walked back to reach the class before the fifth period began.

3

The fact that Radhika was sitting right in front of me made her extremely distracting. I kept looking at the back of her head, trying to deduce things about her. I had read about how Sherlock Holmes picks random details about people and tells so much about them. I thought I could also deduce a few things about her. But I couldn't come up with much.

My joy knew no bounds when the Chemistry teacher made herself unavailable for the eighth period. A substitute period was arranged and Saransh sneaked out to play table tennis. I noticed Radhika's bench partner had gone to the staff room. I had seen enough of him by now to know that he wasn't going to let go of any opportunity to try to impress any teacher at this school. Anyway, as Radhika was sitting alone, I decided to sit next to her.

She welcomed me with a smile. And we started talking. 'So, you want to be an AI engineer, eh?' I asked.

'Yes, I want to be a Physicist and eventually, an Artificial Intelligence engineer.'

'Interesting, but why? Anything related to it that you enjoy doing?'

'Physics,' she replied.

I nodded, but I wasn't fully convinced. I got a feeling there was another answer at the tip of her tongue, which she decided to hold back. We had just met, and I guess she didn't want to open up so quickly.

Just then, a peon came to give a circular to the substitute teacher sitting in the class.

'Can someone read this out loudly please,' she announced. When nobody volunteered, she pointed at Radhika and asked her to do the task.

Radhika shook her head, but the teacher had gone back to correcting the notebooks she had brought along. Radhika realised she had no choice. She walked in front of the class and held the paper. The class slowly grew quieter as my classmates broke off their conversations, looking at her. Her fingers trembled, and she did not look up. I coughed, and as she looked up at me at the sound, I gave her a comforting smile and nodded. Thankfully, she mustered some courage and read the circular in her soft voice.

When she came back to her seat, next to me, the colour had still not returned to her face. I almost wanted to hold her hand and tell her it was okay. I also had a few questions running through my mind, but I didn't want to bombard her and decided to give her some space.

But maybe she read my mind. 'I have a general anxiety disorder,' she said, answering my question before I could ask.

I knew the term, but I didn't know much about it. So, I held back from offering any advice. I could tell that it wasn't easy for her to say. I didn't blame her. In our country, talking about mental health is like addressing a ghost. People would label you 'crazy' at the very mention of any kind of disorder. I felt as if she had confided something that she did only to people who were in her circle of trust.

But at the same time, a tension hung in the

air after she had told me about her disorder. I wasn't equipped to offer advice, but I could try to change the topic and get her mind off the incident that had just happened.

'Do you give money to beggars?' I asked instead.

'What?'

'Do you give money to beggars?' I repeated, as if she hadn't heard me the first time.

'Why are you asking this?'

'I often wonder about the relationship between giving money to beggars and leaving tips at restaurants.'

'What is the connection?' she asked, close to getting a little irritated now.

'Both are activities of giving money where you don't have to. I feel this decision reflects something about us. A waiter at a restaurant is working hard, so he or she deserves some reward. But a beggar might be in dire need of money.'

'But the beggar could be lazy or lying. And the waiter can make enough to support himself.'

'Of course. These are the questions which reveal how you look at the world,' I said.

Radhika thought about what I had just said. And then suddenly, a look of understanding came on her face. 'You said all this to distract me from what just happened?' she said. I nodded and the two of us shared a light smile.

'It was a terrible attempt,' she said and her attention diverted to the notebook on her desk. She was scribbling something on the last page but I knew better than to peep. So I let her be, as I watched the satisfied smile on her face.

When Radhika didn't look up from her notebook for a long time, I started to get restless. I wanted to talk to her more and get to know her. But she was lost in her own world, completely silent. In those long moments of silence, curiosity got the better of me and I finally looked at her notebook.

The first line read, 'It doesn't get worse than this'.

I felt guilty to continue reading and I told myself I shouldn't intrude on her privacy. But my eyes were already skimming ahead to the next line, and by then my curiosity had gotten the better of me and it was too late to stop. I read the next few lines:

It doesn't get worse than this
I try to silence the noises in my mind
But I fail

Why is life so unkind
That I always fail

I try not to think of all the times
I couldn't make it
But I fail

I cry at night but during the day,
I try to fake it
But I fail

Anxiety pierces through me
Making me numb,
not letting me speak

Why can't I just be
Silent and still, not having to speak

The book slammed shut just then, and I looked away quickly, but it was too late. Radhika was glaring at me, although she looked a bit embarrassed as well.

'I am so sorry for peeping,' I said.

'It's not meant for reading,' she lashed sternly.

'But I loved what I read.'

'I don't care. You should have asked for my permission first.'

I decided not to say anything for a while, and give her time to calm down. Eventually, when her fingers stilled on the notebook, I asked, 'Do you write a lot of poetry?'

She still wasn't looking at me, but she nodded.

'That's wonderful. Why do you want to be a Physicist or an engineer? You're truly gifted as a poet. You should work on honing this art. And there are so many ways poets can make money these days. You can write micro poetry on Instagram and earn by collaborating with brands. You can write a book. You can even record podcasts. Lots of people these days –'

'I don't remember asking for advice,' she said, mocking me.

'Arre, but just think about it. The kind of money-'

'Will you please stop? Why do you have to measure everything with money? Why does everything have to be a career? Why can't some things be done just for oneself?'

'I'm so sorry. I didn't mean that.'

'You really think I don't know the things you're saying?' she said.

'I, um, I mean.'

'It's okay. At least you didn't give the other cliche advice I always get.'

'What's that?'

'Oh, you have anxiety. Why don't you go for therapy?'

'Because you already have tried it and it didn't work?'

'Of course. Therapy works for some people, but it definitely didn't work for me. It felt so weird to open up to a random forty-year-old, who has no idea what today's generation thinks.'

I thought about it for a moment. 'Maybe you need someone your age to talk to,' I said.

I am pretty sure she heard me but didn't say anything. Just then, the bell went off, at the worst possible moment. I was waiting for her to respond to what I had said, but she just picked up her bag and left. In between the class's commotion, I just watched her leave, wondering if I had ruined the beginning of a beautiful friendship.

4

A few minutes later, I spotted Radhika at the school's gate. She was standing there, the sunlight seemed to be reflecting from her dark black hair, looking cute in her neutral expression. She was waiting for Jigyaasu to finish talking to a teacher, her thoughts seemingly distant. She was standing by herself and I could tell she was still a little disturbed by our conversation. Guilt gnawed at me for having dampened her spirits earlier, and I was determined to mend the damage I had done.

'How do you go home?' I asked, as I approached her.

'Jigyaasu has a scooter and we live nearby,' she replied, her eyes not meeting mine. There was an awkward silence, as I wondered if this conversation was done as far as she was concerned. But to my surprise, she added, 'What about you?'

'I have a cycle,' I said with a smile. Perhaps, our friendship might be on a ventilator, but it was alive. 'But before that, I have to meet my family at the gate.'

'Your family?'

'Yeah. Do you want to meet them?'

'No, thanks. I'm really awkward around families.'

'But you will love my family. Trust me, they don't bite.'

She reluctantly agreed. As we came out of the gate, a joyful pack of seven or eight dogs came running towards us, their tails wagging furiously. I gave them the Parle-G biscuits that I had bought from the canteen during recess. 'This is my family,' I said.

She bent down on her knees and patted Johnny, my favourite in this pack. His warm brown eyes met hers, and he nuzzled her affectionately.

'He seems to like you,' I told her as Johnny licked her elbow.

'Well, I like him too,' she confessed, her eyes sparkling with newfound warmth.

If there was one thing more important to me than my dreams and ambitions, it was my love for dogs. 'I have many more such friends at Fountain Park. I go there every morning at 6 am,' I shared.

'Oh, *subah subah*? Do you go there to play cricket before school?'

'No,' I replied and said nothing else. I didn't mind telling her about my dream to become an entrepreneur, but this was something else entirely. I doubted that I could explain it without being mocked.

She looked intrigued but refrained from asking more. I noticed Jigyaasu's grumpy face waiting for her impatiently a little away from us.

'Where do you park your cycle?' Radhika asked. 'Which one is it?'

'I keep changing its brand.'

'What?'

'I mean I painted it myself. So, I keep changing the brand name.'

'Now, I have to see it,' she said.

I took her to the cycle stand and showed

her my black ride. 'This bicycle was the first thing I had bought with my own money.'

'Firefox. That's the brand it currently carries.'

'Yeah. I wanted to buy a Firefox cycle but I realised that if I spent that big an amount on the cycle, I would have to delay buying my laptop. But my cycle was going to be my tool, to facilitate my business and I couldn't delay it any further.'

'So, you bought the one you could afford and painted the cycle the way you wanted it?'

'Yeah.' Suddenly, I wondered if the look in her eyes meant she was disgusted by my attempt to pretend that I could afford high brands when I really could not. So I joked, 'This is how poor people can afford branded items.'

She smiled, and I knew she was actually impressed. 'It's prettier than many actual Firefox bikes.'

With that, we said our goodbyes and parted for the day but not before I gave a hug to Johnny and the rest of the pack. I knew Sheru was going to get a whiff and be jealous again.

I thought about Radhika meeting Sheru, my dog some day and what a beautiful moment that would be.

As I reached home, Sheru came running towards me for a cuddle. As usual, he caught the smell of other dogs on me and barked at me. I might be around different dogs throughout the day but Sheru was different. This Indian pariah dog was my heart. I rubbed his head and felt a pang of guilt for not being able to devote more time towards him lately.

My house was a cramped bedroom and a hall, which had a washroom and a kitchen attached to it. Mom and Dad slept in the bedroom while Sheru and I shared the hall. Mom tried her best to make the house look presentable in her limited resources but not much could be done. The curtains needed replacement and the walls had more black stains than the blue paint which had been applied more than a decade back.

By the time I was done catching up with Sheru, Mom already had a plate of dal-chawal ready for me.

'You need new trousers,' Mom said, on seeing its ankle-high length. The grey had also faded so much that it was distinguishable from the white.

'Next month,' I replied. I had thought about it and had told myself that that was the thing I was going to buy next, after the laptop, from my next month's income. I had even decided where I would buy it from. When I had gone a few years back to Unity One Mall, I was enthralled by the rows of sleek gadgets in an electronics store. Ever since, I had dreamt of buying one of the laptops on display. I was very close to fulfilling that great desire of mine.

'You could just ask your father, no?'

'I said I wouldn't,' and I stuffed my mouth so I did not have to answer. The truth was, I could really do with a new set of school trousers, but my last row with Dad had ended with me declaring that I would never take another penny from him again, and I was determined not to go back on that promise, if only to avoid the few minutes that Dad would spend mocking me.

'Beta, there's no harm in asking. He is your father, after all. And you are eating the food he's buying.'

'Trust me, I'd rather not even do that. It's a matter of a few months that I will stop.'

Mom knew it was a heated topic and there was only so much she would prod. 'How was your first day?' she asked as I relished the food. 'And how's Saransh? How come I've never seen this friend Saransh? Have you never invited him home?'

5

I woke up pretty excited. It was 6 am. This was the favourite part of my day, after all. I brushed my teeth, ate a banana, took a shower and headed out with Sheru. It was warm but breezy outside. When I reached house number 52, I rang the bell and waited patiently. I couldn't hear the voice of a single person, but I could tell from the sound that Estella, the golden retriever, was excitedly shifting inside. She was a well-behaved dog and did not bark. I could barely see her on the other side of the iron gate. After waiting for a bit, I wondered if I should ring the doorbell again.

The sun had just come out and people were on their way to the park for their morning walks and jogs. I saw a pair carrying racquets as well. Despite the summer months, the heat wasn't too bad because of the morning hour. Ritu Talwar ma'am finally opened the door. She was one of the most helpful teachers at

Pragati. She was sleepy but made sure she gave me a bright smile.

'How's the dog walking business going, my young Steve Jobs?' she asked.

'Pretty good,' I said and told her I had four more houses now.

She extended her hand and gave me my monthly fee. It was the fourth of the month and I somehow knew she wouldn't forget it. 'Giving you this money every month gives me so much joy,' she said. I smiled back at her. She was not only my English teacher in school but also the reason I had been able to get my foot into this business in the first place.

Once she shut the door, I went to the houses of my other clients in the area. None of them were anywhere near as sweet as Ritu ma'am. Two of them didn't have cash at home and told me they would pay in a day or two. One of them called me 'Chhotu', even though that lady herself was a good one foot shorter than me. Another one told me to take extra care of her dog, even though she herself neglected her pomeranian more than any dog owner I know.

Once the bunch was ready, I focused on my dog children and being excited about the next half an hour I was going to spend with them. On my way to the park, I collected the other four dogs in the area. This had been my morning routine for the past eight months. I had become this block's unofficial dog walker. It seemed to be a much better way to spend my mornings, rather than sleeping in till late or scrolling through my phone or even worse, whiling it away with friends.

Once I was inside the park and far enough from other people, I could now speak to Estella, like I did every day. 'Does your *maalkin* teach you Shakespeare in between meals?' I asked. Estella let out a bark, as if she could understand me and agreed with my statement.

'I wish you could tell me what questions were going to come in the exam,' I told her. It had been more than a year since I had taken any money from my father. I paid for my own expenses and saved the rest of it. For the last couple of months, I had been collecting money to buy a laptop. I needed one to research various ideas for potential business plans and also to maintain Excel sheets of my different projects and income streams. Someday I am going to have a billion-dollar empire. And I want to document every little step that gets me closer to it.

Estella was in a good mood. She kept running around the park, chasing one invisible thing after another. The other four dogs, along with Sheru and I, mostly just followed her along. The park had its usual groups of uncles and aunties. Some kids were playing cricket, probably because their schools had not yet reopened. Within a few minutes, I was completely immersed in my dog world. After all, taking these dogs for a walk was something I enjoyed so much that I'd have enjoyed it even without getting paid for it. In my daytime revelries, I had once wondered if I could charge people money to accompany me on these morning walks. I thought this was quite a therapeutic way of beginning one's day and more and more people should adopt it. But of course, I soon realised it was one of my many wacky ideas which had no substance at all.

Suddenly, one of the other dogs, Monty, barked and started prancing around in circles. I told him how he was being extra mischievous this morning, inspired by

Estella. People find it strange, but I sincerely believe there is nothing wrong with talking to dogs. Sometimes, I even love making up their imaginary personalities and replies. It's fun. As I pulled the third dog, Gabbar, the Pomeranian out of a row of flowers, I saw a face, which I had thought about quite a few times since yesterday. It was Radhika. She was wearing pink PJs with white sneakers and looked cuter than yesterday for some reason.

'What are you doing here?' I asked.

'You mentioned you come to this park every morning, so here I am.'

The realisation of her heightened cuteness made me conscious of my own unkemptness. Of all the places I wanted her to see me, I wasn't sure how I felt about being seen here. I was still getting over being called Chhotu and maybe I would've preferred to have taken a bath before meeting her again. But I could see that she meant to show up as a friend and not to embarrass me in any way.

'Do you own so many dogs?' she asked, her voice almost squeaky.

I laughed and told her that I was just their

designated walker. I introduced her to Estella, Sheru, Monty, Enzo and Gabbar. I told her about the others who were currently not here as their owners had taken them on summer vacations.

'This is the most fun business one could ever start,' she said.

'Calling it a business will be a bit of a stretch. I'm just a dog walker.'

'You're a dog walker? This is worse than opening a chai shop,' an annoying male voice said. I noticed for the first time that Jigyaasu was also there. He was wearing sunglasses. His T-shirt was paired with shorts and long socks, almost reaching his knees. 'So you clean dog shit. I had overestimated you by saying you're going to open a chai shop.'

Estella barked at Jigyaasu as if she understood what he had said. But I realised it was because Jigyaasu was emanating a body language that gave away that he was really scared of the dogs.

'Don't mind him please,' Radhika said. 'He had fallen down as a baby and his brain was damaged.'

'What's your problem with dogs?' I asked

him instead.

'What's my problem? What's there to not have a problem with pet dogs? They take up food resources, which should instead be directed to feeding poor humans. People clean their shit with their own hands and then they have the audacity to say that they have domesticated the dogs, when the exact opposite has happened.'

I was scared by how much sense that made. I felt the pressure of defending my species, but couldn't think of a decent counterargument. Thankfully, Estella barked at him and Jigyaasu took a step back, providing me with a good distraction.

'She doesn't bite,' I said. 'Don't be scared.'

'You really think this is fear?' Jigyaasu said, pointing two fingers of his right hand into his eyes, asking me to look into them. 'I'll tell you what it is. It is a pity for these pathetic animals and what they go through.'

'What do you mean?' Radhika asked.

'What I mean is look at what you have done to this animal. He is tied with a leash which you control. If you left him on the road, he would not know where to look for food except garbage.'

'And that's wrong because?' I asked.

'Because that's not how they were supposed to live. Millenniums ago, dogs were ferocious animals. If they saw a human, they would rip them apart. But centuries and centuries of conditioning has made them these submissive creatures. When I see a docile dog which doesn't even bark, I see centuries of conditioning into believing that they are not attacking by nature. A species which could completely take care of itself now just pouts in front of humans for food.'

'Then why are you scared of them?' I asked. 'This should make you less scared of them.'

'I'm not scared of anybody and never will be.'

'Like I said,' Radhika said, 'Ignore him, please.'

'I've already ignored everything he said,' I replied.

'Why don't you go and complete your ten thousand steps, Jiggy,' Radhika said, clearly trying to get him out of the way.

Her friend understood this too, and for a

moment, he looked like he would refuse. Then he turned and stormed off, with a final parting shot, 'Whatever. I'm going home. Got to get ready for school.'

'What, already?'

But he was out of earshot and it was Radhika who replied with a smile, 'He takes really long to get ready for school. He has a ten-minute routine to just iron his underwear.'

'Why are you even friends with this guy,' I asked.

'So, dog walking, eh?' Radhika answered, totally ignoring my question. 'Looks like you're a serial entrepreneur. I'm glad you weren't bogged down with what happened to BookMyTijori.'

'I would have done this even without the money. Getting paid for chilling with dogs is just a bonus,' I replied.

'Your love for dogs is a romance that Jane Austen will be proud to have written.'

'I'll be happy to be interviewed by this Jane Aunty or whatever her name is.'

'How did you even get this work?' she asked.

'It wasn't easy in the beginning. These walks were mostly done by people's domestic helps.'

'Oh, that can be a terrible idea,' Radhika said.

'Exactly. I was infuriated by how bad they were at taking care of the dogs. They were just not interested in making sure that the dogs were having a good time.'

'Did you try talking to their owners?'

'I did but they just didn't see my point,' I said. 'And gaining their trust was always going to be a challenge.'

'It's almost like they are giving their children to you. They can't just trust a stranger off the road for it.'

'Yeah. But luckily, on one of my morning walks, I saw Ritu ma'am.'

'Our English teacher?' she asked. Everyone knew Ritu Talwar, she was one of the most popular teachers at school.

'Yes, the same one. Estella is hers. Even though she loved Estella, with her hectic work hours, she was not able to take care of her dog that well.'

'What about her family?'

'She lives alone,' I said. 'That's where I stepped in. When I spoke to her, she appreciated my spirit and became my first client.'

'And she must have lobbied for you after that?'

'Of course. It was much easier once Estella's mood showed clear improvement. And here we are, with a loyal customer base. And Sheru gets a big friend circle as a bonus.'

'Sheru is your dog?' she asked.

'Yes, Sheru right here, is my brother.' Sheru came running towards us on hearing his name. He jumped on me, with his paws on my chest until I rubbed his belly and showed my love for him. He noticed Radhika and positioned himself in a way that indicated how he needed her to rub his tummy. I was reminded of the thought I had had just a day ago about Radhika meeting Sheru. I couldn't believe it had come true so quickly.

'I can see why some therapists keep dogs,' Radhika said.

'Why do they?'

'They are called therapy dogs. Rubbing Sheru is proving so calming to me, the act of touching a breathing chest is so relaxing. This would work on anybody.'

I wondered if my business idea of having people join me on these morning walks had some merit after all. But I couldn't imagine it. It felt like one of my dumber business ideas.

'You're truly getting paid for what you love. That's the sign of a great business,' she gave a thumbs up.

'Like I said, calling it a business will be a bit of a stretch.'

'Netflix used to rent DVDs. We all start somewhere.'

It had been less than 24 hours since I met her. But I don't know how she just knew the right thing to say to me. I was a little embarrassed about how unscalable this business was. There was not enough money in it for me to hire other dog walkers under me. It was just enough to cover my current money needs. But this was a gateway till I found my real business idea. I liked that it made me interact with rich people. If I had to make money from rich people, it was important I knew them and got to know how they think.

It wasn't a big park, but the walking track served the purpose. It was mostly deserted because of the heat these days, with some couples sitting under a few trees. Radhika and I were now walking beside each other with the dogs in front. I was holding them all by the leash.

Just then, Sheru deviated from the track and started moving towards a bush. I assumed he had sniffed something he wanted to eat or chew, as he often did with litter. But instead, we heard a girl's shriek from the bush. Sheru had sniffed a couple who were looking for privacy behind the bush and startled them. I pulled the leash in the opposite direction, as the couple refused to come out because of embarrassment.

'Behave yourself, Sheru,' I said.

'He is a real cutie, isn't he?' Radhika giggled and said, looking at Sheru. 'Where did you get him?'

'Oh, it's a long story.'

'We have time, 30 minutes or so,' she nudged me.

'He was just a few days old when he was hit by a car near our house. I was on my way to the nearby market when I spotted him on the side of the road. He was bleeding all over and his face was badly hurt.'

Radhika gasped in horror and patted Sheru's head even more affectionately than before.

'I used the jute bag that mom had given me to put the groceries and vegetables, to wrap and hold Sheru. I did not know any vet, but thankfully, I knew where the nearest clinic was and it was open. The doctor's initial reaction was denial because he was not a veterinarian doctor. But then, it was a slow work day and he could see the puppy was badly injured. So, he decided to try his best with whatever tools he had,' I shared.

I still remember that day vividly and the pounding in my heart as I saw the bleeding puppy by the street. I was in 6th standard and had no idea what to do to help him. But I just knew I couldn't leave Sheru like that.

At the same time, I had a bigger problem:

my father. I somehow knew that he would be opposed to the idea of having a pet. But the puppy did not make a single sound at the vet's and I believed I'd be able to hide him somehow. I kept him in a box under my bed and covered him in an old shirt.

All my efforts were in vain. When he sat down to watch TV, the puppy wriggled out from under the bed and barked softly but loud enough for Dad to hear. 'What is that dirty dog doing under your bed?' my father said.

I tried to explain, but he would not listen to a word. 'There is no space in the house,' he said. 'Take it back outside.'

'He's hurt, he won't survive,' I said. I already knew that his only concern was money. Usually, when we fought over money, I gave up as soon as he made it clear he would not indulge me in whatever I requested. This time, I would not budge. This was not just a fancy t-shirt or higher-quality notebook. I had already grown attached to the puppy.

I'm not spending a paisa on it. Are you still so childish that you don't realise how hard it is to earn money? As if we don't have enough expenses already, now you're bringing in another mouth to feed, and a sick thing too.'

'I'll use my pocket money. You don't have to do anything.' Finally, he relented, with some muttered prediction that it wouldn't survive a night.

I replied, more to myself than to him, 'He will survive. He's not a dog. He's a *sher.'* In my head, I started calling him *sher* and that's how he went on to get his name.

I couldn't even sleep the first night after bringing him home and would lean under the bed to watch the rise of his chest, afraid he would be dead if I didn't keep a constant watch. But I gradually got used to it. I'd feed him milk, apply medicine and check up on him throughout the day. Every night I slept, I worried if he was still going to be able to move the next day. When I left for school, I wondered if he would still be alive when I returned home. My thoughts were all scattered and I would be the first to leave the classroom, cycling like a madman with no thought for my safety.

My mother gave me some more money, but I refused. My father's words had gone too deep for that. I watched over Sheru as he slowly raised his head with his eyes so full of trust. Right then, I decided that I would make enough money that I'd never have to turn a blind eye to a needy life or spend on whatever I wanted. There was no point in working so hard if I could not fulfil my own desires.

Gradually, Sheru's wounds started to heal and I found my closest buddy in him. His one eye made him somehow cuter than most dogs, and he would turn his head this way and that when searching for me. Saransh had jokingly said that if a building caught fire and it had Saransh and Sheru in it, I'd probably save Sheru first. I had laughed, but in my heart, I knew that was true. No human friendship could possibly measure up to the blind loyalty he displayed.

'I'm glad he is adopted and not bought,' Radhika said.

While talking about Sheru, I realised that I felt a certain sense of protectiveness towards Radhika too. I wanted to help her in overcoming her anxiety issues. I was not one to give medical guidance, but I wanted to be there for her as a friend.

'I was wrong about you,' she said.

'What do you mean?'

'I'm sorry about what I said yesterday that you measure everything with money. You have a sensitive side too. You just don't let it come out that often around humans. Only dogs bring it out.'

I wasn't sure if I liked the label of being 'sensitive'. 'I don't know about all that. I just know I love dogs,' I said.

'I believe this is your superpower. The way you connect with dogs is quite rare. This will take you somewhere.'

I stared at her, a little dumbfounded. Nobody had ever talked about me this way. I was always the guy nobody noticed or cared for. Every word she said was absolutely true and made me feel something inside my chest.

Radhika and I walked together, as we had some way to go before we had to head separate ways to our homes. I was dragging my cycle and enjoying the silence. I must have ground my teeth on seeing something and Radhika noticed it.

'What happened?' she asked.

'I just saw a stationery shop which was shut,' I replied.

'So?'

'It angers me a bit to think the shopkeeper hadn't opened up yet, missing the chance to sell to school children who would need to buy something on their way to school.'

'Do you often have thoughts like that?'

'I can't help but obsess over business. It's like an Extra Class in my head, which never gets over.'

'Look around you,' she said. 'What else pops out for you about entrepreneurship?'

'Can you see that astrologer? The board says he charges twenty rupees per horoscope reading. He would actually get more customers if he charged 500 rupees. People are more willing to pay five hundred than twenty.'

'You're really different, Yogesh.'

'When I walk into the school corridor, I hear everyone talk about distant European footballers, nonsensical internet celebrities and pointless restaurants. I just can't relate to them. I feel like I should hold them by their shoulders and tell them that none of it mattered. The European footballer they spend hours every day fawning over would not help them move ahead in life. Instagram celebrities with seven image filters on their faces are only giving them complexes about themselves. The stand-up comedians are trying to spread awareness about mental health issues but end up glamourising the same because of their limited understanding.'

I realised that Radhika was taken aback by the passion in my voice. I had to stop. This was not a normal 7 am conversation.

'I know what you mean,' Radhika finally spoke, a bit quietly. But then she continued, her voice picking up confidence. 'For most of our class, every clothing brand's seasonal sale is a major event. They may or may not visit a temple on a Tuesday, but visiting Starbucks thrice a week was unmissable. They knew the universe of mobile games to a greater detail than they knew their own neighbourhood. Every day, they typed three times the number of words on WhatsApp than they actually uttered from their mouths.'

She trailed off, and she looked a little

surprised at her own long-winded reaction. I was surprised too, and couldn't believe that this girl, whom I had only met, had so much more depth to her than I had thought at first. I wished it wasn't time to leave, but we had to leave for school in around an hour. But the good news was that I was going to see her again in school.

6

The moment I reached home, I saw my father having *aloo parantha* for breakfast. He looked at me with a stern face.

'How was cricket?' he asked.

Dad didn't know I used to work as a dog walker. If he actually saw that I could barely hold a bat, he would be quite shocked to see how slow a learner his son was.

'It was okay. I scored 31 runs, but we lost the match.' Over the last few months, I had made all kinds of stories to convince him of my passion for the sport. Dad had made it clear very long ago that he thought my dream of becoming an entrepreneur was something he didn't approve of.

'That's okay. The point is to have a little fun.' I sat down, a little surprised. My dad was in a good mood apparently, otherwise, he'd have laid into me for even losing the match. He seemed to be in a preachy mode, because he went on, 'Beta, playing cricket and all is fine, but remember that you cannot afford any distractions right now. Becoming a software engineer is not an easy thing. '

My father had decided my career path for me way before. To him, my dreams were also merely a distraction, useless noise in my head. Part of the reason might also have been the fact that he doubted my capability. There was no polite way to say: He thought I just didn't have it in me. He had never explicitly said it. But I knew. He went on, talking about how hard it was to get a job.

'The rich people have it all easy.' As a union leader, his job was to be a thorn in their flesh. 'I work in 35 degrees Celsius every day on the factory's shop floor, just to get food on the table. I don't want my son to do that.'

I wanted to leave the room as quickly as I could. '*Achha*, Dad, I have to go,' I said, and rushed for a bath. Maa hurriedly fed me a bite of *aloo paratha* before I left for school.

One of the reasons why I am friends with

Saransh is because he balanced my intensity with his lightness. Where I took everything way too seriously, he was not easy to fluster. He also knew exactly when to turn on his obnoxious comments and distract me whenever I was overthinking something. As we sat on the last bench, watching student after student enter the class, Saransh took one look at me and knew I was upset. And he resorted to his favourite technique to cheer me up: commentary.

'Just see how everyone thinks the new year will be a new slate for them,' Saransh said. 'They think about all the times they goofed up last year or did something uncool. And they promise themselves that this year onwards they will be smarter and more popular.'

I wanted to believe Saransh was an idiot, but what he said made sense as well. So, I just nodded silently.

'I call this the "New-lusion Syndrome". That's right, I invented that term. Everybody gives themselves some version of that same "new year, new me" cocktail. But what they forget is that they are still the same person, with the same IQ, with the same apprehensions and the same insecurities. That is why, by the third day of the session, the same old

pecking order gets established. If one was a goofy, insecure, obnoxious bully, he would go into the same role. If one is an insecure geek who never shared his notes, he would go back to being the same. People change but the character remains the same.'

We were constantly looking at the door, watching students come in. When Radhika entered the class, she waved at me. Along with Jigyaasu, she sat down on the same seat as yesterday - right in front of Saransh and me. And of course, it led to a mischievous grin on Saransh's face.

'Why was Radhika smiling so much? Or should I call her *bhabhi*?' he whispered. I smacked the back of his head and asked him to shush. I told him about the morning, which was easy fodder for more leg-pulling.

'*Ek din mein itni gehri dosti*,' he whispered to me.

'Hush!' I said, worried that she would hear me or worse, Jigyaasu. But Saransh would never shut up just because I asked him to. So, I continued in a whisper, 'It's not like that. We just connected over a few things. And honestly, I was also surprised to see her at the park.'

'Who tells a girl to meet at the park? We are not in the 8th standard anymore. Take her to Haveli Hookah Parlour, *na*. It's a popular dating place. Even college students go there,' Saransh suggested.

'No, thanks.' I chose not to point out that it was not a date.

Just then, Gajendra Mishra entered and started taking our attendance. After that, he began teaching us about Kinematics. I was mostly zoned out through the lecture. But I do remember hearing the word 'velocity' at least 20 times.

Nothing extraordinary happened in class until recess. Jigyaasu was sharing his *dabba* with two other toppers in our class. Saransh had already left for his *marampitti* league on the playground. Radhika came up to me and asked me to accompany her to the canteen like yesterday.

'I am glad I came in the morning,' she said. 'Otherwise, I would have missed a perfectly beautiful morning and of course, meeting those absolute cuties. Sheru has my heart.'

I nodded, as I didn't know what to say. She took a cheese sandwich and a cold coffee. This time, we sat on the staircase outside the canteen. I saw quite a few pairs of eyes looking at us. But I ignored them. I don't remember spending so much time with anyone other than Saransh at school. I didn't mind my own company and I did believe having too many friends can distract me from my future goals. But I'd be lying if I said it didn't feel good to have a new friend.

'So, when did you write your first poem?' I asked her.

She thought hard for a moment. 'I.. I don't remember, to be honest,' she said.

'Then it must have been a long time ago.'

'Maybe. All I know is that poetry has been a part of my life for a long time.'

'I can tell it's important to you. You should seriously think about pursuing it.'

'Oh, don't you start again…' she trailed off.

'Okay, okay. But if you ever feel like showing some of your poetry, I'd love to read.'

'I'll think about it,' she said with what looked like a suppressed version of a smile.

I remembered Saransh's suggestion of taking her out somewhere.

'Hey, would you like to come to Goyal Juice Center with me after school?' I blurted without thinking.

I regretted it immediately. We had met in the morning and then, now. I shouldn't have asked. It was classic clingy-boy behaviour.

'Cool,' she agreed.

I was shocked. 'Umm, alright then,' I said. 'Let's meet at the gate after the last period.'

'Okay. Jiggy usually drops me home. I will ask him to pick me up from Goyal Juice Center on his way back then.'

'Sounds great,' I said as we got up to go back to class, trying my best to act calm. Suddenly, I was one of those people who hung out at juice shops after school. Who was I?

When I told Saransh about my after-school plan with Radhika, he spit out the water he was drinking.

'A girl agreed to meet you after school and

you're taking her to a juice shop. If not a hookah place, at least take her to a coffee shop?'

'It's not a date, man.'

'Then what is it?'

'It's just two people going somewhere to talk,' I said.

'Oxford Dictionary literally defines a date as two people going out to talk.'

I was going to ask him when was the last time he even opened a dictionary. But our Mathematics sir came in and the class became silent. While the Math lesson by Gupta sir was somewhat interesting, Neena mam's Chemistry lecture almost put me to sleep. I was desperately waiting for the clock to tick and the last period to get over. When it did, Radhika and I exited school from the back gate to take the shortcut. As we crossed the market, I noticed for the first time how deserted it was. I had taken this route a few times before with Saransh but somehow never paid attention to the surroundings. The juice shop was small and cosy and had walls painted in bright yellow.

'Cute place,' Radhika said.

For some reason, her approval of my choice made me happy. Four rather noisy men were sitting at the front table. They were talking about God knows what, but they were extremely loud. We steered clear of them and took a seat on the extreme opposite corner.

I ordered a lemonade and she asked for a mint watermelon juice. Our token number was 12.

'You're my first friend at Pragati,' she declared.

'What about your Jiggy Viggy boy?'

'Haha, he's been my friend since we were born. He doesn't count.'

'Twelve,' shouted the man from behind the juice counter.

I was getting up to go and fetch the glasses, but Radhika insisted on going herself.

I noticed that after taking the tray from the man, she kept it back on the counter and carefully picked and returned the plastic straws. As she turned around to move towards our table, she accidentally bumped into one of those rowdy loud men, who was walking to the billing section. Some of the juice spilled over onto him.

'Are you blind?' the guy said rudely and walked off.

I hurriedly rushed to her and took the tray. I was carrying the beverages or whatever remained of them, to our table when I realised Radhika wasn't next to me. She was still standing at the same spot where the accident had happened. She looked like she had frozen. I kept the glasses and went back to her. She was breathing heavily. With sweat breaking out of her forehead, she looked like she was going to throw up. It seemed like a more intense episode of the anxiety attack she had while introducing herself to the class.

Without wasting any time, I offered both my hands to her. After a few seconds, she took them. Now I could feel many more eyes on me. But I told myself not to feel embarrassed, as I had something more important to be done.

'Radhika, listen to me. You're okay,' I said as she held my hands tightly. 'It was just an accident and that guy was an ass.' She didn't move and said nothing. Her face was pale and her eyes looked slightly watery.

'Okay, look at me. Don't pay attention to anyone else. I want you to pay attention to your breath. Focus on each breath, alright? Just try to inhale slowly.'

After a few moments, her breathing started slowing down.

'Good, now, continue holding my hand and let's walk towards our table. Okay?' I said.

She nodded and started taking small steps with me. As her steps grew more confident, she also seemed a little embarrassed as some onlookers were staring at us. As we settled on our seats, I gave her a glass of water and asked her to take a few sips. We drank our beverages in silence for a while. Once I was sure the storm had passed, I initiated a conversation that I had been meaning to have.

'I have an offer for you.'

She looked a little confused. 'Huh?' she said.

'Hear me out. Yesterday, you mentioned that talking to older people about your issues makes you uncomfortable. Maybe you don't relate or connect to them. But you and I, we do have a connection, right? You even called me your friend today. So, let me help you.'

'So, you're saying you want to be my guiding light, my therapist, my saviour?' She was mocking me, again.

'No, I am saying I can help you, as a friend.'

'Okay,' she said.

'That was easy,' I was surprised.

'You don't seem like the type who gives up easily. So, I thought, why waste time arguing when I know you will find a way to convince me eventually?'

'Smart girl!'

'That I am,' she smiled.

I felt relieved to see her smile again.

'Okay, so it's a deal. Today, I am hereby appointing myself as your Life Coach.'

'Life coach?' she raised her eyebrows. 'I thought you were helping me as a friend.'

'From this moment, I am going to be your full-time friend and part-time life coach,' I declared and gave her a high-five.

She high-fived back. So our deal was on.

'Our first session will be tomorrow at Fountain Park.'

'What makes you think I will come there again tomorrow?'

'You will,' I said.

It was already close to 3 pm. We paid the bill and left the juice centre. As we stepped out, we noticed Jigyaasu coming towards us riding a blue scooty. He parked it a little ahead of us and waited for Radhika to hop on. He didn't greet or acknowledge me. But he also didn't pass any mean remarks, so that was a first. Radhika looked at me with a hint of what looked like gratitude in her eyes. Maybe I was overreading her expressions, but it did look like a silent 'Thank you' to me.

7

The next morning, when I rang the bell at Gabbar's owner's house, Aunty opened the door immediately. 'Come inside,' she said. I closed the main gate to ensure Sheru stayed on the lawn and went in. This was the first time I had entered the house. Usually, Aunty or their house help brought Estella to the lawn outside their home.

I looked at the expensive crockery kept in the showcase in the house and thought about how Aunty had chosen to exchange money for keeping these shiny porcelain cups and plates in their living room. I looked at the biggish vase next to the sofa, the chandelier on the ceiling and the transparent table and thought about how all these things used to be money. I looked at the lazy air in the house and thought about how all this money used to be people's time, which they had exchanged for money. The paintings on the wall looked pretty-ish but didn't make sense to me.

When Aunty didn't come out for more than a few minutes, I sat down on the sofa and waited for her patiently. Estella came running to me and jumped on my lap. I patted her and continued looking around. After almost 10 more minutes, Aunty came out and gave me my money. I thanked her and left.

'Come, Estella, let's go.' I called out excitedly.

She wagged her tail and followed me obediently. As the two of us stepped outside the door, I heard the Aunty call her house help. 'Rama, that dog guy sat on the couch. Please have the covers washed today.'

An entrepreneur has to die a thousand deaths before he or she makes it. These insults were mine. She didn't mind the dog sitting on the sofa. But the dog walker sitting on the sofa was a problem for her. Her words stung me. But I knew better than to react. I knew what I was doing this for, and had already told myself that this was just a temporary measure until I got my big idea. I just held my head high and strolled away towards the park. It was a bright and sunny day and a little hot already.

Unlike most days, playing catch with Estella, Sheru, Enzo and others didn't have the same cheering effect on me. The more I tried to forget Aunty's comment, the more it played on my mind. Just then, I saw perhaps the only sight which could have cheered me up. It was Radhika's face. Of course, Jigyaasu was behind her as well.

Radhika had brought treats for all the dogs and all of them rushed towards her. The same air which had moroseness hanging in it till a few minutes back now seemed cheerful. That's the effect she had on most spaces she entered. Jigyaasu maintained his distance from the dogs and pretended that he needed to jog away.

'As much as I love seeing them, why did you call me?' she asked.

'Yeah, so, it's time I put on the Life Coach hat again. I want to teach you a grounding technique. I want you to practise it whenever you feel anxious again,' I told her.

'I am listening.'

'It's called the 5-4-3-2-1 method. Working backward from five, use your senses to list various things you notice around you. For instance, you can mentally start listing five things you see, four things you can touch and feel, three things you can hear, two things you can see and one thing you can taste.'

I had spent the whole night reading about anxiety and ways to manage it. The grounding technique seemed to be a common one recommended by many therapists across the world. I had watched tens of videos on YouTube to make sure I understood the finest of nuances involved. But as I spoke, she shook her head and continued playing with Sheru as if she hadn't heard a word of what I had said.

'What?' I asked.

'I am 16. Not 12,' she snapped. 'As someone who has battled with anxiety for more than four years, what makes you think I don't already know about this? It doesn't work on me.'

She was right. She knew a lot more about anxiety than I did. She had been there, done that. It was probably what the forty-year-old therapist had tried to teach her in the very first session. I realised I'd have to be a little more creative as a Life Coach.

'Okay, let's scratch that lesson.'

I heard her giggle. I realised she wasn't paying much attention to me anyway. She was busy playing with her furry friends. I joined them. After a while, Jigyaasu returned from his sprint and stood in a corner, maintaining a safe distance from the dogs.

'I think you'll be a fine Life Coach to me. You found Sheru and nursed him back to life. You helped me yesterday when I had an anxiety attack. You have a knack of helping others recover. I am sure you will find a way to help me feel better,' she said.

'Thank you for believing in me, ma'am.' She probably realised that this time I needed some reassurance.

She patted Sheru as he nibbled on her white shoes.

'No, Sheru, come here,' I said, afraid he was going to spoil her footwear.

'It's okay, I don't mind it. He's too adorable.'

'That he is. He is not a fan of being out when it's too sunny though. That's why he is a little annoyed today. He prefers coming out only in the evening.'

'An animal who's afraid of one of the most basic elements of nature: the sun,' Jigyaasu said in a mocking tone. Perhaps, he was feeling left out and needed to make his presence felt, as he walked closer.

'Let me take a picture of him,' Radhika said and took out her phone. I think he was warming up to the idea of dogs around him. Radhika clicked a photo of Sheru and Jigyaasu peeked at her phone while she did so.

'Cute, *na*?' she asked him.

Not the one to be pleased easily, Jigyaasu denied.

'Anybody can point at the dog's face and click a button,' he said. 'Why don't you put in some effort and use some creativity?' Jigyaasu took out his phone and pointed at Sheru. As Radhika and I watched, Jigyaasu appeared to be busy creating some artwork on his phone. When he was done, he showed his screen to both of us.

Radhika couldn't help laughing out loud. Jigyaasu had opened an app with a dog filter and put it on Sheru. So now, on top of Sheru's regular nose and ears, there was another dog nose and two more bigger dog ears. Sheru also had sunglasses in the dog filter. He looked even more adorable than before.

'Oh God, the sunglasses look so cute on him,' Radhika said. 'Maybe you should get him a real pair.'

Jigyaasu thought that was funny, but something struck me upon hearing that statement. I stopped walking. In fact, I stood still, trying to divert all my attention to that one important thought that had just crossed my mind.

When I suddenly caught the brainwave, I almost screamed, 'Oh. My. God.'

Radhika and Jigyaasu looked puzzled.

'That is the idea I had been waiting for all this while. This... This is brilliant. It was right here, in front of me, all along, but I could never see it! Goggles for dogs. How come the thought never crossed my mind? I mean, look at Sheru. The thing he needs right now more than anything else is a pair of sunglasses, but nobody is making them till now. Dog owners would do anything to make their dogs look cuter. You have no idea how many dogs across this country are suffering because nobody is making sunglasses for them! Oh my God. This is my billion-dollar idea, this is what I needed.'

'Yeah, and I will make shoes for dogs,' Jigyaasu said, but he was completely ignored. Radhika didn't know how to react. The idea probably sounded like a joke to them, but the fact was that I was dead serious about this.

'Are you sure?' she asked. 'I mean, I have seen dogs wear sweaters and collars, but I have never seen dogs wear goggles. Do you think dogs really need sunglasses? I mean, I'm a human and I've never bought sunglasses for myself.'

'What makes you think people know what they need?' I said. 'People don't know what they need until you tell them what they need. Look at his phone. You really think people knew they needed a phone with a touch screen until Apple told them they needed a phone with a touch screen? Or apps with random filters?'

'Let's just think about it for a while,' Radhika said.

'Why do you keep doing dumb things in the name of business?' Jigyaasu said. 'Why don't you make some app or some e-commerce website? This is the stupidest idea I have heard in my life.'

'It has all three elements,' I said, having completely tuned out everything around me. 'There is a need and there is a gap in the market and my knowledge of dogs would give me an unfair advantage. Everyday when I take Sheru for a walk, every third girl stops and plays with him and I've always wondered if there was something I could do to make Sheru stand out from other dogs. I would pay good money for it if I had it.' I might have seemed delusional to them, but I knew I was onto something. I even had a name for it. Doggles.

'Are you okay?' Radhika asked.

I was not okay. I wanted to finish the walk, run home and start work immediately. But I was responsible for the dogs. I finished their walk earlier than unusual, said bye to Radhika, dropped the dogs off at their respective places and rushed home. My mind was racing so fast, I didn't know where to begin.

8

The first three periods of the day were a blur. I was too excited to understand any words coming out of any of the teachers' mouths. I was just sitting on my seat, constantly scribbling in my notebook. Every now and then, I could feel Radhika's eyes on me, but I made sure I didn't meet them. I was so tempted to vent all my thoughts to her, but at that moment, I needed to focus. The last thing I wanted was to have my train of thought broken by how calming her smile was.

Before the fourth lecture, I snuck out and went to my favourite corner of the school. It was the lab assistant's room in the Physics Lab. Ved Prakash sir, the aforementioned lab assistant, was there. Everyone called him Veepi behind his back, but I got to call him so on his face because of our friendship. Veepi barely existed for most students, but for me, he was a very good friend. Because of his meek demeanour and underdog smile, people underestimated him. But I looked at him as a wealth of knowledge and my first sounding board for everything that bothered me. The experience of BookMyTijori had brought us closer than anything else. He had gone through a month's suspension because of me and hadn't shown even an iota of anger towards me.

Veepi had very little hair on his head for someone who was not even thirty. When he smiled, he gave the impression that some of his teeth were missing too. But when I looked properly, I realised it seemed so because of how uneven his teeth were. He had the most unthreatening demeanour about him, someone who always wanted to help everyone. His limited mental faculties made most of the students not take him very seriously. However, for me, he made a great bouncing board for all my crazy ideas.

'Chai?' Veepi asked as soon as he saw me. He had a secret stove hidden in his room and we had chai and Parle G biscuits together quite often. The school had assigned him a small room in the lab, which was also the place where I carried out my little entrepreneurial experiments. It had all the equipment an inventor could need. But most importantly, it had a desktop computer.

'The smile on your face is broader than usual,' Veepi said and sucked his own saliva, as he did after uttering every single sentence.

'I've got *it*,' I said, with a broad smile.

Veepi knew what I was talking about. I had spent hours and hours in front of him, blabbering about how desperately I needed a billion-dollar idea. Only finding that could bring a smile like that on my face. I explained the whole plan to him. Ever since it had come to me, I had been in a state of euphoria. It seemed so obvious. I took out a notebook and scribbled some designs on a piece of paper.

Veepi knew what he had to do. His role was to help me think through the execution of my idea. He contributed with what he could think of:

You can design it this way…

I think the cost of manufacturing will be somewhere in the range of…

The market size for such a thing will be at least…

Instagram will be *very* important...

Getting an investor will be a piece of cake...

Our conversation was interrupted by a knock on the door. It was Radhika. 'What are you doing here?' she asked.

'What are *you* doing here?' I asked her back.

'When I didn't see you in class during the fourth period, I asked Saransh where you'd be. He told me where to find you.'

'Oh,' I said. My thoughts suddenly went to how I looked at that moment. My tie was loose and my hair was probably all over. The notebook in front of me had all kinds of scribbles. And I might have had a hint of craziness in my eyes as well. I must have looked like a mad scientist to her.

'You look like you should take a break. Let's eat?' Radhika said after looking at the notebook in front of me.

'I think I'm not going to take a break for a few years now,' I said, totally forgetting about the *chole-rice* in my bag that Mom had packed in the morning.

'I understand,' she said. 'That's why I took the liberty of going through your bag and brought your lunch over here.'

I don't know what Veepi sensed on seeing this, but he excused himself. 'I have to go to the staff room to have lunch with Gajendra sir,' he said, in a very non-convincing way.

'But what about your lunch?' I asked Radhika.

'Will you not share yours with me?' she said and blinked innocently.

Radhika and I had the whole Physics Lab to ourselves.

'Will you make me your executive assistant?' she said, taking a bite of chhole-rice.

'I don't think I can afford you,' I replied.

'Well, I'm not that expensive. I'm going to need a glass of juice every week for my services.'

'But I don't even have work to give you yet. I don't even know what to do,' I said, as I put the last bite of lunch in my mouth.

'I will be your research assistant. I will figure

out whatever you need figured out. Cost of sunglasses material in Somalia. Seven thousand and thirty dollars per ton,' she said, as she faked typing quickly on an imaginary computer.

'I have to brainstorm on some designs. Why don't you research some designs on Veepi's desktop and help me?' I said.

Radhika loved her first task. I could see that she really wanted me to succeed. That was just what I needed beside me. I got a little lost in my own design scribbles in my notebook. Suddenly, I looked at sunglasses quite differently. I saw its curves and details in a much deeper way. My train of thought was broken by Radhika when she let out a very audible gasp.

'What happened?' I asked. There was shock on her face and she was struggling to describe what she had seen. I looked at the desktop screen and it had Google on it. Radhika had searched 'Goggles for dogs' and a bunch of results had shown up.

Of course, the business already existed. All good ideas were already taken. Obviously, someone had done this before. Suddenly, it seemed quite obvious. Why the hell had I not searched for this simple thing since morning? Now, I was staring at tens of Amazon links with designs that I could never match. It was probably a very mature industry, which had multiple international companies competing in. How could I assume this was an unchartered territory?

'Like I said, you need a break,' Radhika said, keeping a hand on my back.

9

I did something I had never done before: I faked a stomach ache and went to the medical room to lie down for the rest of the school day. I wish I could say that I needed to think over some things, but the truth was that I didn't have it in me to face Radhika or even Jigyaasu, for that matter. He was right. It was a stupid idea and I should perhaps think of some app idea like everyone else. I lay still, moving very little, hoping that the bell for the final period would never ring. I needed the privacy that only the medical room could offer in the whole school.

As I was lying down, I heard a sound I didn't expect. The medical room had a quiet white Labrador. The moment I saw it, my eyes lit up. I had never imagined seeing a dog in our school's medical room. Just then, I spotted the person responsible for the medical room. It was a young lady doctor, wearing a white lab coat, who looked friendly.

'What is he doing here?' I asked.

'You mean Dobby? Dobby is a therapy dog. I'm the school counsellor as well and I thought it would be a good idea to use a therapy dog with students.'

'What on earth is a therapy dog?' but it struck me that Radhika had told me about the concept, as soon as I finished saying the sentence.

'Well, a therapy dog is a dog that is used to give love, affection and comfort to people whose touch bank is low,' the counsellor replied.

'Touch bank?'

'Yeah. We humans need a certain amount of touch to function properly as people. Children get it from their parents. Grown-ups get it from their spouses. But when a person doesn't get this required level of touch, their stock needs to be replenished. And that's what a therapy dog does.'

'Wow, this is so cool. Come here, Dobby,' I said and somehow the dog responded to it. I wished I could see Dobby in a Doggle, but that possibility seemed slim at that point. Patting him made me a little better for a few minutes, but the sinking feeling in my chest was way too deep. I knew the comfort I felt when I played with Sheru and walked the dogs, but I did not think that the mere act of hugging a dog would give me so much calm.

The way time works, the final period's bell eventually rang. I waited for a while, for everyone to leave. I just wanted to see my dog family and be in their presence for a while. By the time I reached the school gate, everyone had left.

There was no stress that rubbing my hand on Johnny's tummy could not relieve. He came running towards me like he always did. I suddenly felt a little better. Just then, I noticed that someone had been standing near a tree and looking at me. Of course, it was Radhika.

'You have way too many hideouts in this school,' she said.

I couldn't smile back at her. 'Happens when you go to the same school your whole life.'

She caught on to my mood and crossed her arms. 'Are you going to remain this sullen boy for the rest of the year now?'

'Why don't you find someone else to laugh

with you for a bit?' I snapped. I realised immediately that I should not have said that. After all, I was still her Life Coach. Moreover, it was basic human decency to talk properly. She had waited for me, in spite of the heat. She was only trying to make me feel better. 'I'm sorry, I didn't mean to -'

'You think you're the only one with problems?'

'I said I'm sorry. I really didn't want to -'

'You know what your problem or maybe even your biggest strength is?' she said. 'It's that you're always in obsession mode. You just don't know how to be less intense or take something lightly. Learn to relax and enjoy a few things.'

'What do you mean?'

'So what if some people are already selling what you want to sell? You think Facebook was the first social media site? You think Google came up with the idea of search engines? You think the iPhone was the first phone? So what if others have made what you want to make? You make your own. If humans can have sooooo many brands of sunglasses to choose from, why can't dogs have a few?'

This was the first time I had heard her say something with so much passion and conviction.

'But —'

'But wut nothing. Just because one company already exists, it definitely doesn't mean there is no space for another one. Who better than an absolute dog lover to design better sunglasses than what is already there? No one can match your hard work and sincerity as well. You must work like a madman like you already were.'

I nodded.

'Flipkart was not the first company to sell books online. But they were the first *in India* to do so. Similarly, you can be the first one to sell dog sunglasses here,' she said matter-of-factly. The truth was that she was right. There could definitely be space for another player in the market. And to be honest, the designs that I saw were definitely terrible.

'Just focus on how you can do your best,' she said. 'Stop thinking about what others have done.'

I agreed. And wondered how this girl knew the exact right things to say. 'You're right,' I said. 'The international products are imported and hence are overpriced for an average dog owner. We'll make stuff which even a Yogesh can buy.' It felt strange to address myself in the third person, but Radhika knew exactly what I meant.

Radhika was right. And she was wonderful. Within a few minutes, I was back in my obsession mode. I knew I had a lot of work to do. We decided to go to Goyal Juice Center, to discuss the way ahead.

As we left the premises, I said, 'I'm beginning to wonder who is whose Life Coach.'

'I was your friend, that's all,' she smiled.

I knew she was simply being modest, so I played along. 'Yeah, you didn't really do much at all.'

Her eyes widened. 'What?'

'Yeah, I think that therapy dog Dobby did most of the work of making me feel better. Just a few moments with him, and I felt good as new.'

'Well, I was right about therapy dogs, wasn't I? If I knew about Dobby, I'd have suggested that you spend some time with him.'

'Yeah,' I said, more seriously this time, as she had brought up the topic that had been on my mind. 'I actually did not give much merit to the idea when I heard it from you. I knew dogs were great, but I didn't think they could be so effective in lifting someone's spirits up. But Dobby changed my mind.'

'The same goes for your Doggles idea. There are things about it that you may not see, but you can do so much more than what is already done.'

She always said things that made me feel a little more alive than I usually did during other ordinary moments. 'How can I repay you for all your wisdom?'

'Get me some lunch,' she said. 'I didn't bring any.'

'Why do you never get it by the way?' I asked, remembering that she never actually brought a tiffin box to school. She always went to the canteen or didn't eat at all.

She sighed and said, 'My mom… My mom is not around.'

'Why, where is she?' slipped out of my mouth.

'She… she…,' Radhika trailed off.

I realised I had done exactly what I had been so careful about. I had triggered her by asking about her mother.

And in the middle of the deserted market that we had crossed the previous day, she froze. There were no operational shops or people around. It was an abandoned old *bazaar* between our school and the actual market. I needed to act quickly and make her feel better.

'Okay, Radhika. You're now with your Life Coach Yogesh, not your friend Yogesh. Tell me one thing, can you trust me and do as I say? I promise it will help you feel better,' I said, once we reached the empty road. My words somehow managed to break her out of her spiral. She looked like she wanted to retaliate, but she kept mum and nodded instead.

'I want you to scream, as loud as you can.'

She stared at me like I had said something utterly bizarre.

'The thing is,' I continued, 'we keep a lot of emotions bottled up inside us all the time. So, it's important to let them out every now and then. This is just one way of doing that. I understand you're reluctant, but just trust me and go for it.'

She didn't really look fully convinced. But she did it, she screamed. But her voice was barely louder than her usual volume. I signalled her to go louder. She took a deep breath and in a few tries, her sound was deafening. Just as I had wanted it. And then she did it again.

'Kaun hai wahan?' shouted a middle-aged man from a shop at the fag end of the lane. He looked like he was taking an afternoon nap there.

'Did that boy do something,' asked another old man who joined him. They were walking towards us in a hurry.

That was our cue to leave. We didn't really decide, but Radhika and I held each other's hand and ran. Those men ran behind us for a few seconds, but they couldn't keep at it and gave up. Phew! A girl screaming in a stranded market. A boy next to her. I joined the dots. How did this possibility not cross my mind before?

Once we reached closer to our school's front gate, we spotted some familiar faces of other students from our school. Some of them were enjoying their post-school hang-out and two girls from our class were munching on some road-side candy floss. We were back on our home turf.

Then we looked at each other and burst into laughter.

'*Abbe yaar*, that was not supposed to go like this!'

Radhika was still giggling. 'Don't worry, I enjoyed this exercise.'

'It's called Scream Therapy. And I knew it would have a positive impact on you.'

'Okay, don't get overconfident now. It was not cathartic or life-changing or anything. But yeah, it did make me feel a little lighter. Followed by the adrenaline rush of the run after that, this made for a great exercise overall.'

'I am glad I finally got something right,' I said.

'And you ended up making me feel light,' she smiled. 'In my hour of fright, I found a friend so bright. Now, all I need is a bite, let us quench this blight.'

'Wow, you made that up right now? Of course, you love poetry. Only a poet can talk like that.' And we started off down the road. I steered us to a detour so we would not encounter the same two men we had run away from.

'I am not a poet, Yogesh. I just happen to like poetry. I find comfort in Emily Bee's words and sometimes I scribble some stuff of my own.'

'Emily Who?' I asked.

'Emily Bee. She is my favourite poet.'

'Where can I watch her poetry?'

'Watch? Funny how when we think of poets now, we think of video instead of books,' Radhika said.

'So, she has published a book?'

'Yeah, she has.'

'Can I borrow it from you? Do you have it?' I asked.

A car blew past us, honking so hard I nearly couldn't hear her response. 'No.'

'Did you check it in the school library?'

'Yeah. I finished reading the whole poetry shelf already. The thing is that Emily wrote the book way before she was famous. So, the publisher did not publish too many copies. I have tried so hard to get my hands on it. But I just couldn't.'

'Hmm,' I nodded. We had reached the juice shop by now and went in. There were far more empty tables than the last time and I was glad for the quiet. We went up to the counter.

As we waited in the queue, she said, 'Who is your favourite poet?'

I knew that she was expecting me to say that I don't read poetry and I didn't really like anyone. But I had an answer for her. 'My favourite poet is Elon Musk,' I said.

For a second, she thought it was a joke and that I would follow it up with the name of Jaun Elia or Faiz. But I meant what I had said.

'But Elon Musk is not a poet,' she said.

'For me, a poet is someone who is capable of understanding my deepest thoughts and deepest desires better than anyone else. And the person who understands humanity's deepest desires and aspirations the best, according to me, is Elon Musk. So that makes him the best poet alive, according to me.'

Radhika was taken aback, but she smiled at me. 'What you just said is poetry itself,' she said.

'Well, coming back to your poetry, when can I read some of those scribbles? I remember telling you already that I'd love to read your poetry someday!'

'This pineapple juice is so good *yaar*,' she changed the topic. 'Just what I need after screaming in public.'

Jigyaasu came to pick her up a few moments later and off she went.

10

'Jab bhi dekho phone pe laga rehta hai,' my dad's baritone voice shook me out of my reading mode.

I was scrolling through my phone, trying to learn more about the random exercise I had made Radhika do on a whim.

'Do you even know that one can study on their phone too?' I fought back.

I was sitting in the living room in peace when he came in and spoiled my mood. Sometimes, he came in the afternoon to grab a quick lunch before going back to work. It was one of those unfortunate days.

'I know very well what kind of studies happen on the phone. Your generation is totally ruined. Do us the favour of picking up a book and studying at times,' he continued to scold me.

'Jaane dijiye,' Mom intervened, coming from

the kitchen. 'You've come all the way to eat. So have it while it's still hot.'

'You don't always have to be his advocate and save him. He is a grown-up now and needs to start taking responsibilities,' he shut her down.

My nostrils flared as I stared at my father. I don't remember the last time we had seen eye to eye and spoken like a regular dad and son.

'I've not taken a single paisa from you in the past year. I pay for my school, I bought my own cycle and I take care of Sheru's expenses. So don't teach me about responsibility,' I finally said.

'I never refused to give you money. Don't forget it is because of my hard-earned money that you started going to school in the first place, you thankless moron,' he shouted.

I had had enough. There was no point arguing with a man who refused to listen. I mentally tuned him out, went inside and banged my door shut. I put on my earplugs and played an episode of my favourite startup podcast, 'My First Million'. Listening to it was my favourite form of pick-me-up when I felt down. It not only diverted my mind but also motivated me.

'*Ladki mili toh bhai ko bhul gaya*,' popped Saransh's message on WhatsApp. I wanted to be irritated, but there was an element of truth in what he had written. I really hadn't seen much of him in school all day, which was rare. So, I stepped out of the house and called him.

'*Bhai*, I watched this Marvel movie and it was so good. You should watch it,' he said as I answered the call. 'Actually, you should take Radhika *bhabhi* for that movie. Girls are loving it,' he added.

'Stop calling her that, *yaar*. We are just friends.'

'Yeah, friends who hang out pre-, post and during school hours,' he teased and then asked, 'Where did you go after school today?'

'Nothing much. Just made her scream.'

'You made her what?!?'

I realised immediately what Saransh must have imagined on hearing I made her scream. I had to take corrective action immediately before his fantasies could go wild. I told him about Scream Therapy and what Radhika and I did at Goyal Juice Center.

'My mom screams all the time,' Saransh joked. 'Why is it not having any positive effect on her?'

'By that logic, even my dad should be stress-free,' I laughed too.

After that, we discussed how he had started going to the gym. It had been two days, but he could already feel his biceps growing. I realised I hadn't told him about Doggles at all. I didn't expect him to understand, but I told him anyway.

'That's great *bhai*. Girls love entreprenununu,' he said. 'I'm with you. I will be your CFO who gets caught in some scandal like tax evasion or something. People will think it's because I'm a genius, but it will actually be because I'm just an idiot who doesn't know tax laws.'

Saransh could never pronounce the word 'entrepreneur'. And yet, he never chose to say businessman or any other equivalent of the word and I found that hilarious. 'Just the encouragement I needed,' I said. 'If you were here, I would have kissed you right now.'

'Thank God, I am not there then,' he chuckled. 'Save it for Radhika *bhabhi.*'

I didn't know why, but his words made me blush. I could visualise kissing Radhika for a moment, but I shoved that thought aside. There was no time for romance in my life, all my attention was reserved only for dogs and Doggles. Besides, I had forged a great bond with her as a friend and I didn't want to jinx it.

When Saransh and I finally hung up, I proceeded to read up on other companies that manufactured goggles for dogs. I wanted to make Doggles look different from what was already available in the market and also something that wasn't too complicated to manufacture. As I gathered every bit of information, I imagined myself sharing it with Radhika, and somehow it made the whole process much more joyful.

11

When mom called me for dinner, I quickly ate two *rotis* and some *aloo-palak*, played a little with Sheru and went back to my room.

Just then, I noticed my phone was blinking. Was Saransh calling me again?

No. It was a WhatsApp message from an unknown number, 'Hi'.

There was no display picture. And I didn't want to waste my data in looking up who this was on Truecaller.

I didn't think much of it. But then, the sender sent an image. When I downloaded it, it turned out to be a photograph of a page from a notebook. It had something handwritten on it. I knew immediately who it was.

Sheru chews on shoes and shreds the mail,
Leaving messes without fail.
Yet, in those eyes, a glimmer of affection,
A troublesome charm, a unique connection.
For though he tests our sanity,
In his eyes, there's sincerity.
Annoying, yes, but love prevails,
In wagging tails and furry tales.

'That's the sweetest thing I have ever read,' I replied.

'I wrote this the first time I met Sheru.' There was a smiling emoji and a dog emoji after that.

I read the poem again. One can just tell when the emotion in words is real.

'How are things with Doggles going?' she sent another message.

'I don't know. I'm feeling a bit stuck. I'm wondering what my next steps should be. Nobody seems to be taking me seriously. Yesterday, I was telling Saransh about the idea and it was as if I was myself rejecting the idea while telling him because it just sounds so ridiculous coming out of my mouth.'

'It's not a ridiculous idea and you know that.'

'I do, but how do I make others believe the same?'

'Maybe instead of telling people about it, maybe you could show them a piece or something? It would be a lot easier to believe if you had an actual sample in your hand, no?'

I chewed on the idea. In theory, it made sense, but I knew it was not a joke to create a piece. 'But how would I? It's not like I have a plastic moulding machine lying in my garage which I can just fire up?'

'Yeah, but there must be some *jugaad,* some hack through which you can create something. You're the creative one among the two of us.'

'I don't know anyone who has that machine,' I said.

'See, the first pieces don't have to be finished products. You just need something which proves to people that this is something which works and not only that, also how it looks.'

'Yeah, but how do I do that?'

12

'I'm going to lose my job because of you,' Veepi said, with the most forced smile possible. If it was anyone else in his place, he would have shouted and scolded me. But Veepi was too sweet for that, which was why I could take my liberties in taking his help.

'Relax, nothing is going to happen,' I assured him. I had skipped the morning prayer assembly and showed up in Veepi's laboratory. I wasn't sure if the Physics Lab would be open already. But I found Veepi sitting and watching a Kapil Sharma comedy video on his phone.

It was time to start making some samples. Sunglasses are made of three parts - the frame, the temple and the lenses. I could figure out the lenses at a later point, once I had the other parts ready. For the time being, I just wanted to get the frame right. I needed to melt some plastic and turn them into thin sheets until they became malleable and then cut them with a steel cutter.

'I need a good quality cutter,' I asked Veepi while sitting on my usual seat in his room and commenced my work. When the bell rang, I looked at the time and realised that not just the assembly but even the first period was over.

Veepi entered the room and whispered, 'You're going to get me in trouble,' as some students started coming in. 'The 12th standard students are here for their class and the teacher is going to ask me what you're doing here.'

But as I had said, nothing happened. A few students had seen me before I had closed the door. But they didn't seem to care much. I continued working without paying any heed. I hadn't managed to do anything concrete though. Another period went by as I experimented with a couple of elastic bands. I tried to figure out the right level of stiffness or elasticity. But after a point, I started feeling a little lost. I didn't know where all this was going. I was clueless.

Everything that could have gone wrong went wrong. I burnt my hand, cut my finger with a scalpel and damaged several plastic sheets while working with them. I just did not have an artist's hands. Veepi kept trying to tell me to use safety tools, but they would have made me even less precise. The harder I tried, the worse I worked, until I reached a point where I couldn't do it anymore. I didn't have a craftsman's skills and it brought me to the verge of tears out of frustration. I hadn't slept a blink the previous night and had been at it since morning. I kept my head on the table and shut my eyes.

'Umm, hello?' I heard Radhika's voice.

I jumped up in alarm, as I realised I must have fallen asleep. I noticed the door was open and Veepi was winding up the residue of the experiments that had been done by the previous batch. I realised it was time for recess. Four periods were over and I had made zero progress.

'I knew I'd find you here,' she said. She was carrying a big shopping bag for some reason. I looked at it quizzically and she answered the question in my eyes by emptying the entire bag on Veepi's table. What I saw made my heart thump against my ribcage. I reached out to steady myself against the table, as my legs felt a little wobbly. I also wanted to hug her.

'YOU ARE A GENIUS,' I shrieked.

There were several pairs of sunglasses lying on the table. I counted around twenty, some dulled with age. I had no eye for sunglasses, but even I knew that these were fairly expensive. Their metal designs were sleek, and shone even now, against the weathered wooden tabletop. Some of these had delicate cat-eye frames, and a few pairs shared an aviator style.

I cursed myself for not being able to think of it before. But my happiness trumped every other emotion at that point. I also felt thankful for having Radhika in my life.

'Last night, after our conversation, I had an epiphany. How about you use human sunglasses and alter them in your designs? It won't be ideal, but it would be some progress?'

I didn't know what epiphany meant, but I was not the poet in that room. So it didn't matter.

'I don't know how to thank you,' I said.

'Friends don't thank each other, how many

times will I have to tell you?' She patted my back and I sat up in surprise. But she was staring at the sunglasses and said nothing more.

'Who do these belong to, by the way? Hope no one will turn up tomorrow, calling me a *chashma chor*,' I joked.

'Don't worry about that.' She was laying them out and examining them and she looked a little upset. 'These belong to someone who will never show up, ever.'

I knew then that they belonged to her mother.

I went through the sunglasses one by one and identified eleven usable pairs. I discarded all the aviators, as there was no way they could be made to fit a dog's face. I also discarded an old wayfarer. I had been obsessing over how a human being's face is different from that of a dog. To begin with, the nose bridges of these glasses were too big for dogs. So, I would have to cut that bridge and paste both lenses closer together. The stick which held the glasses needed to be taken out completely and replaced by some sort of elastic.

From the shortlisted ones, I picked a pair of blue-collared sports goggles as the first one to work on. But as earlier, my hands weren't as neat as I wished they were.

'You're really bad at this,' Radhika said.

'I was always the worst in arts and crafts and I never realised that that would become an obstacle in my entrepreneurial dreams.'

'Get aside and let me do it,' Radhika said. 'Just tell me what you want to do.'

Where I was a train wreck at this, Radhika was a natural, as her hands moved with great ease. Some lenses were lightly scratched in a couple of places, but that didn't matter. We started fidgeting and trying different things.

I tried to help where I could, but mostly I just sat back and watched her work, only joining in when she told me to help her with something. I had to admit that I was enjoying working with her–I usually had to handle everything related to my business by myself, even when I wasn't good at certain parts of it.

'Where did you get these elastic bands?'

Radhika enquired, picking up the pair she was working on.

I was replacing certain parts of the sunglasses with elastic to make the goggles a bit more dog-friendly.

'Oh, these. I took them out of the waistbands of some of my old shorts at home. I knew I could put them to use somehow.'

'Impressive.'

Radhika also didn't return to class after recess and accompanied me. Less than a week old at Pragati, she was already bunking classes for me. Working with her felt easy and natural. The pairs in our hands started looking somewhat like what I was aiming for.

'I should have paid more attention in those Art and Craft periods,' I said.

'Every millionaire is not an artist.'

'Every artist is not a millionaire,' I responded.

'True, but artists mostly don't run behind money anyway,' she stated.

'Who doesn't run behind mon—'

'*Yeh lo,*' Veepi entered the room with a burner from the chemistry lab on the floor above. He also gave us a hacksaw from his own toolbox and a better scalpel, from the biology lab. I thanked him and he shut the door and left. Radhika and I ended up using each of those tools for something or the other. Within half an hour, multiple prototypes were ready.

We stared at them in silence. They looked more scratched than before, and the elastic bands sat oddly on the lenses. I had to admit to myself that they didn't quite have the glamorous look I was hoping for. But they looked perfectly functional, which was all I wanted. I just needed a prototype to test on dogs.

'I don't think I've ever made prototypes for any of my ideas,' I said. She said nothing, and I looked at her. Her head was cocked sadly. 'Come on, don't tell me you don't love the sight of them.'

'I love them because I made them,' Radhika said, 'so I am a little biassed. But they don't really look that good, na? Some even have scratches on them.'

'This is not how the finished products will be, *baba*. As you had already said, these aren't ideal, but they sure show some progress. Just decent-ish is enough right now. I only needed an example to showcase the potential of Doggles. And we've multiple. So this is great actually,' I explained.

'Oh, yay. And here I was thinking all our hard work might get wasted.'

'Nah, hard work never gets wasted, we are good,' I offered her a high-five. She high-fived back.

I didn't want to disappoint Radhika, so I held my ground in front of her. But even I knew the prototypes didn't look good. In fact, they were borderline ugly. But at least they were functional. That was a start. These could be tested somewhere and I could collect feedback on them.

As Radhika got up from her seat, she said, 'So, which dog is going to be our first model?'

13

When the teacher left after the seventh period, Radhika and I quickly sneaked in before the next one started.

'You've come today?' Saransh asked. 'I thought you stayed home to work on Doggles. Where have you been since morning? Veepi's room?'

I nodded, as I slid into the desk.

'Oh, so that's why Radhs *bhabhi* vanished post recess. I am guessing she was with you too.'

I told him how she had been a huge support for me through everything in the last couple of days. 'I can't really explain in words how talking to her feels. But she makes me feel like I am already on my path to becoming a billionaire. She always knows the right things to say. Just her presence comforts me,' I kept blabbering when I noticed Saransh's face.

He had a naughty grin plastered all over. That is when it struck me for the first time. Was. I. Crushing. On. Her? Oh, God. Was this happening?

'Finally, it's happening, *yaar*,' Saransh said, with a smile so broad, it was almost creepy. 'You finally have feelings for a girl. I was beginning to worry your dick doesn't work.'

'I know what you're going to say. But I'm not going to confess anything to her.'

'And what genius explanation do you have for doing that?'

'I've just started work on my billion-dollar idea. The last thing I want is a huge distraction,' I said.

'You are calling your biggest support your biggest distraction? That's just dumb.'

'Suddenly, you're a feminist?' I said, but what he said wasn't completely baseless.

It was hard for me to concentrate during any of the classes after that. And for a change, it wasn't Doggles that I was thinking about.

I looked at her, sitting three feet away from me. She was looking at the blackboard, as our Math teacher, Gupta sir, talked about set theory. Her nose was wrinkled and I could make out she wasn't able to understand most things. Her almond-shaped eyes looked even larger as she tried to comprehend everything the professor was saying. Her hair was tied into neat braids, but some stray strands of her hair fell carelessly on her face, making her look even more adorable.

A part of me wanted to lean forward and kiss her. Holy shit. My heart was racing and I didn't really know how to navigate through these brand-new feelings rushing through me. I was screwed. This was really happening. For years, I had told myself I was different from most boys. But I guess what they say is true: Those who think they are different from others are most likely to be like others.

It was like my lungs had forgotten the rhythm of the normal breathing process, a task they had performed with no challenges for my whole life. My breath suddenly felt laboured and unnatural. What now?

14

'Take a left from ahead,' Radhika said. We had borrowed Jigyaasu's scooter and I was the one riding. I had initially been a little worried because I had never ridden a scooter before. But being a gearless vehicle, it wasn't very different from my cycle.

I had no idea where we were going. After school, Radhika had told me that she wanted to take me somewhere and she had arranged for a ride for the same. I wanted to go home and work on Doggles, but I was currently incapable of saying no to her for anything at all. Moreover, she seemed to have put in a lot of effort already in arranging the scooter.

As I parked, I saw the board in front of me. 'Tails & Tales'. It was the dog cafe that I had read about many months ago. I had researched them when I started my dog walking business. At some point, I had plans to promote my dog walking services here, but I had never actually ended up coming here.

'I told you I wanted to see some dogs wear our samples,' Radhika said, as she got off.

During school, I had thought it would be a piece of cake to find dogs to sample on. Immediately after the eighth period, I played a little with Johnny and his dog family and tried to put my Doggles on them. At one look at the Doggles, though, Johnny moved away from me. When I held him in place so that Radhika could put the Doggles on, he shook his head vigorously and once even barked at her. The other dogs seemed to be equally repulsed by the sample.

The fact that I couldn't see a single dog with our sample had disappointed me and Radhika had decided to turn my mood around. She said, 'I'll show you a better place we can try. And the dogs' owners will also be there, so we can take their input.'

'Tails & Tales' turned out to be the happiest place I had ever been to. It was a safe space where not only rescued dogs but also the fancy ones, who visit pet spas every week, played together. It reminded me of Sheru hanging out with Estella and others.

The well-lit cafe was filled with the smell of freshly brewed coffee and frolicking dogs, two things that I had never imagined could go so well together. Not a single cushion or chair was out of place and the walls were pristine. A Great Dane approached me curiously and sniffed me all over. He probably caught the scent of Johnny and the other dogs, for he began to bark. An old lady looked up from her iPhone and examined me from head to toe.

I wondered what I must look like, dressed in an old school uniform and sweaty. It was the sort of place that Gabbar's mom would come to and where I looked completely out of place.

'You think people will let us make their dogs wear these?' I asked Radhika.

Unlike me, Radhika seemed a lot more at ease. 'There is only one way to find out,' she said and looked at me expectantly. When I didn't move, she extended her hand, signalling me to move. Talking to strangers was not my forte. If it wasn't for my beloved business idea, I would never even consider it. I walked up to a burly man with a handlebar moustache. In his lap, a poodle was licking at a cup of dog ice cream.

'Hello sir, these are Doggles - goggles for dogs. *Aap inhein pehenke,* I mean, *pehnaake dekhna chahoge*?'

'What?'

'Goggles for dogs,' I said again and I could feel the other woman with the iPhone watching me. My confidence began to fade.

'Is this a prank or something?' the guy said. 'Don't waste my time with such nonsense.'

Seeing his angry face, I thought about just apologising and walking away. I looked at Radhika and she signalled me to keep trying. 'No, sir. I'm an entrepreneur–'

He burst into laughter, so loud that the poodle froze in shock. 'Finish your high school first. You think anyone will take you seriously when you're still wearing a uniform?' He stood up and walked off. '*Pagal kahin ka,*' I heard him murmuring.

Radhika looked shocked. 'That jerk,' she said. The whole cafe had gone quiet and I saw more than a few heads turning our way. Radhika glared at the old woman, but then her face went pink and she turned to me. 'Look, let's change our approach. How about a more upbeat and positive note? Use more vibrant words. And these people in South Delhi love to show off.'

Secretly, I told myself not to approach people who looked like they needed some classes on anger management. So, I looked around and saw a lady passing by with an adorable golden retriever. She didn't look like she would yell at me, so I walked up to her.

'Wow, is that Louis Vuitton?' I asked a lady, who looked at me suspiciously for a second. But the moment she understood what I was saying, a smile came on her face. 'It looks so wonderful. And the brown colour matches your dog.'

'Yes, I bought it on purpose for that reason,' she said eagerly.

Radhika knelt down. The dog lifted his paw for a handshake and she laughingly shook it, tucking her hair behind her ear. 'He looks so cute,' I said. 'I bet he'd look even better with one of these goggles.'

The lady looked at the prototype that I was holding. Her expressions gave away that she didn't really like them. 'These are the latest rage in Milan from what I hear,' Radhika said, which was enough to convince the lady.

I knelt down as well and gently held the dog's head. He fussed for a bit and reared his head back. But he was much better behaved than Johnny and his friends. Radhika soothed him with a dog treat and while he was happily munching on that, we slipped the Doggle over his head.

The effect was immediate. For a moment, no-one spoke. 'Wow,' Radhika said softly. A surge of fierce joy rose within me. The retriever looked infinitely cooler. 'I can imagine him on a magazine cover, posing like he is a pilot or something.'

The dog stuck his head up and barked and the light glinted off the dark lenses. 'I'd almost buy one of these,' the woman said, petting the dog eagerly. We just stood there, admiring the way the dog looked. He obviously loved the attention, for he began to run around the cafe. I heard the click of a phone and looked up to see the woman with the iPhone putting her phone down. She had taken a picture of the dog. It suddenly struck me that everything at the cafe had come to a halt and everyone was looking at the dog with Doggles. It almost felt like if I had some pieces ready, people would pay me money at that very spot.

The hair on my arms was standing erect now. That was the moment I had been waiting for. This was it, I thought to myself. For the first time, I felt like I belonged in this South Delhi cafe. My father would be forced to admit he was wrong after all and all the jeers I had endured would finally be worth it.

Radhika nudged me and I blinked, coming back to reality. 'Not so stupid after all, huh?'

I couldn't help but grin. 'I never said it was stupid, remember? That was you.'

'I'm going to pretend I heard you say thank you. You're welcome, by the way.' She stood up. 'And by way of thank you, let's have some fun with these dogs.'

The rest of the time we happily spent playing with the dogs. The dog seemed to have taken some peculiar interest in me and kept poking at my chest and arms. Radhika had found a cocker spaniel that did not stop barking except to breathe and sometimes lick her face.

'How about some juice?' she said after wiping down her cheeks of saliva.

I got up at once. This would be on me, as a way of showing my appreciation, I thought to myself. I walked up to the counter, and my heart sank.

The cheapest drink was for 120 rupees. I was very particular about filling petrol in Jigyaasu's scooter for a hundred rupees. That, along with this order, would postpone my plan of buying a laptop by at least a week. I could get a chai for 10 rupees by the wayside. But the Doggles trials and Radhika's company. It was all worth it.

As the sun began to go down, the scene at the cafe changed. Suddenly, the ambient music paused and people started clapping. I hadn't noticed a mini stage in front of us till that moment. A well-dressed guy was standing there with a microphone. I noticed his blue and white Nike shoes and admired them.

'Welcome, everyone. For the uninitiated, Tails & Tales hosts an open mic event every week. We've had a stand-up comedy night, we've had a spoken words session. Today, it's all about poetry. Without further ado, let me call our first poet of the day - Miss Prerna Sharma!'

A girl came on stage and took the mic from him.

Returning home after so long,
I was afraid

I'd made many promises,
but let them all fade

The woman of her words,
I wanted to be

But when I meet them,
what would they see?

I took a few steps,
but then I froze

What happened to my
'Baat karenge har roz?'

As they looked into my eyes,
another tear rolled down

All they saw was their
favourite class clown.

'That's my time, guys. Thank you for being a

lovely audience,' said the girl after finishing her poetry and went off the stage.

People on the tables around us started clapping and cheering for her. I clapped too. I noticed Radhika shifting a little in her chair, looking slightly uncomfortable.

'Wasn't that great?' I asked. Radhika only nodded.

The smart guy returned. 'That nearly brought tears to my eyes,' he said. 'I hope it inspired some of you budding poets. How many of you are already into poetry?'

Radhika's hands stayed down, but I was fresh with my success with Doggles and knew how much she had helped me. The least I could do was return the favour. I raised my hand and the man pointed at me. I waved at him and gestured to Radhika.

'Not me, her,' I said. 'She writes really well, too.'

'A school student, how lovely,' he said. 'Come on, then, let's hear you.'

Radhika had leaned back into her chair like she wanted to disappear into the cushion. She darted a furious look at me. 'Why did you do that?' she said. 'Why are you trying so hard to embarrass me?'

'C'mon. Just read any of your tens of masterpieces,' I said, confused. 'I spoke on your behalf. Now, all you need to do is read the poems you've written.'

'Yogesh, you don't know anything about social anxiety,' she said angrily.

'Come on, miss,' the man said. 'The stage is waiting for you.'

Radhika looked so terrified I thought she'd faint. I leaned forward and said in a whisper, 'Look, you don't have to if you don't want to.'

'I already said I don't want to.'

She tried to wave at the man on the stage to indicate her lack of interest, but the man said, 'Looks like she needs some encouragement, everyone.' And he began to clap. The gesture was taken up by the others sitting around. I had just raised my hand to ask for silence, but it took a few seconds for people to register my request.

Radhika was losing her cool and she got up and walked out. The audience fell silent abruptly at that moment. I wanted to rush after her, but there was a bill to be paid. I made the payment and rushed out.

She was standing in the parking lot, next to Jigyaasu's scooter, staring blankly at the ground. 'Do you have Paytm? I will send you my share,' she blurted out as soon as she saw me.

'You can pay for me too, in that case,' I smiled.

She said nothing.

'Come on, *yaar*. You got dozens of sunglasses for me today, helped with Doggles, came all the way here and even gave me advice on how to approach the dog owners. The least I can do is pay for that juice.'

'Mocktail,' she corrected me. We stood in silence, and I knew she was building up to saying something. We spoke at the same time. 'I'm sorry–' I said, but I didn't really know what I was apologising for.

But she wasn't done. 'Look, I don't write poetry for an audience. I do it because writing is the only way to help me deal with my emotions. Would you share your deepest thoughts with some strangers?'

I didn't think I'd have any trouble gabbling on about my entrepreneurial dreams to any stranger willing to listen, but looking at her face, I thought that she was talking about something else entirely. 'I didn't realise that's how you feel. I still think talking to strangers will help you with your anxiety because you don't have to care what strangers think even if you do mess up, but I won't force you to do anything you don't want to.'

'Okay.' She smiled. 'So are we paying for that juice or what?'

'Mocktail,' I said, and she laughed.

15

'Where are we going?' Radhika screamed through her helmet as I rode Saransh's scooty.

'You will see,' I said.

'I have to be back home by eight, no matter what,' she said.

The anguished look on her face had eaten away at me and I badly wanted to cheer her up before we parted ways for the night. It didn't take me very long to hit upon the perfect plan, as I had already organised a surprise for her.

'You will be, don't worry. This won't take much time.'

'Tell na, where are we going? I don't like surprises, Yogesh.'

'You will like this one.' I was confident.

We rode in silence for the rest of the journey.

But the sound of the breeze mixed with all the honking on the streets somewhat sounded like a background track that plays when they show India in one of those Hollywood movies.

We entered a narrow lane and I carefully parked the scooty there. Radhika got off and gawked at the board in front of the cosy little store that was there.

'Narendra Library,' she read out loud and looked at me. Even though she seemed a little puzzled, her excitement was pretty damn evident.

I spotted Narendra Uncle sitting at his usual spot, a high stool near the entrance. Clad in *kurta-pyjama* and his trademark black-rimmed spectacles, he was engrossed in a book. He is around 70 years old, but he looks like he is 60 at best. I've never seen him without a book or at least the day's newspapers in his hand. He loves reading and the tiny store that also doubles up as a library was his retirement home. There was a kitchen and a room attached behind. He had once taken me back there for some *chai*-biscuit.

His face lit up as he saw me.

'How are you, Yogi *beta*,' he asked.

'*Badhiya*, uncle. Hope all's well with you too.'

He nodded and noticed I had brought company. I introduced them and they exchanged a few pleasantries. Once we entered, I took Radhika to the corner I knew she'd love. She already looked like a kid in a candy shop. Even though there was hardly any space to comfortably move around, she seemed to be in her comfort zone. There were no other customers around.

And then I showed her the shelf I was waiting for her to see. 'A dedicated poetry shelf,' she exclaimed with joy.

'Yes, Narendra Uncle himself likes to read a lot of poetry,' I told her.

'The library in Pragati doesn't have a good poetry section,' she complained, without looking at me.

'I'm glad you're happy,' I said.

'Nothing makes me happier than a poetry bookshelf. Neruda, Rumi, Robert Frost, Sylvia Plath, they're all here,' she said with a certain twinkle in her eyes that I had never seen before.

'They even have Rupi Kaur,' she rolled her eyes. 'This is like a treasure box for every poetry lover.'

'Yes, but sadly, very few people know about this place,' I said.

'How did you discover it then? I never pegged you for much of a reader.'

'Oh, hello. What do you mean? I have read exactly seven and a half out of syllabus books in my life.'

She smiled.

'A few months ago, I came to this gully to purchase my cycle. That's when I saw a book on this store's display rack. It was called, "The $100 Startup," and I felt like reading it. I ended up spending the next few hours here. I finished it on the same day but didn't buy it. But Narendra Uncle didn't say anything,' I shared.

'What about the other six and a half books?' she questioned.

'I bought three of them here and rented the rest. Currently, I have a rented copy of 'Zero To One' lying at my home. But I haven't had the time to read it amidst dog walking, school, and now, Doggles.'

'Wow, so you read, *haan*?'

'Yes, all thanks to Narendra Uncle. He opened this place with his life savings after retiring from a government clerical job. I really respect people who build the life of their dreams on their own, no matter what their age is.'

'It's a beautiful place,' she said.

I didn't tell Radhika about the business idea I had had with Narendra Library. I had realised that school seniors didn't think twice before giving away books to their juniors. I realised that these old books might have been worthless for the seniors, but there were definitely people who would pay money for them. And then a thought crossed my mind: What if I collected old books from these seniors and sold them to those who would pay at least some money for these books? I wasn't proud of that business idea as it almost felt like a scam. I refrained from telling Radhika about it. The last thing I wanted was to lie to people to take their books.

'Here, I want to show you this particular

book on this shelf,' I said, pointing towards the book I had traced with so much effort in the last few days.

'WHAT? Nooooo,' said Radhika. Her eyes had a blinding twinkle as she saw what I was pointing at. It was Emily Bee's book.

'Here,' I gave her a copy of *Broken On The Outside*.

A few days ago, I didn't even know a book like that existed. But after reading about Emily Bee, I knew all about it. Radhika was ecstatic as she opened the book and realised it was a signed copy. There was 'Love and Light' written on the first page along with Emily Bee's signature.

She hugged me. Tight.

I hugged her back. Apart from my mother, I had never hugged a woman before. This was different, *wayyyyy* different.

'Thank you for bringing me here,' she whispered to my right ear. I felt her breath on my neck and a shudder rocked through me. She continued, 'Emily once said in an interview that the poetry she wrote for this book was her most honest writing as she did it before she got fame and had a career.

She wished she could write with the same innocence that she wrote in this book. I've been looking for this book for years and never found it.'

'It wasn't really that hard,' I lied. 'All I had to do was search for it.' I decided not to mention that it had taken me many days of effort and frantic calls. I had even visited Ansari Road and Nai Sarak in Old Delhi looking for it but had found no luck. It was only the experience and network of Narendra Uncle that he had talked to some importers who had a copy lying around in one of their godowns. Just the previous evening, he had messaged me that the copy had now reached his library.

'Still, it's almost a collector's item. I tried everywhere but could NEVER get hold of it. Not on Amazon, not on any website or library,' she went on.

A part of me was registering everything she was saying, but another part was doing cartwheels in my mind. Her oval-shaped face was glowing more than ever and I felt like it would fit perfectly in my cupped hands. As I stared admiringly at her, she continued to be lost in her own trance. She smelled Emily Bee's book deeply and turned the page. Then she softly read out the lines she had been waiting to read on a hardcopy for a long time.

Body of a woman, grey hills, white lilies,

You look like an animal, but one with a soul.

She continued reading for a while and I let her.

'Thank you,' she said, when she finally looked up from the book. 'Thank you for this.'

'Don't you know the basics? Friends don't say thanks,' I repeated the line that she had once thrown at me.

She laughed.

16

'What a missed opportunity,' Saransh said as I narrated the previous evening's entire story to him. The two of us were on our way back to our class after the morning prayer assembly.

'Huh?'

'Huh *kya*? The library was the perfect setting for your first kiss. You should have made a move, duffer.'

I wanted to tell him to shut up, but somehow the words didn't come out. The truth is that he was right. I had spent the whole of last night thinking about that moment. It would have truly been a perfect first kiss. And honestly, I felt it in my bones. It felt like the right thing to do, to ask her if she wanted it too. But I couldn't risk our friendship for it.

'She doesn't know I like her. And as I've already told you, she will never come to know either,' I said.

'So you want to be her Jigyaasu part 2? A buddy *bhaiya*?'

'*Abbe yaar, bhaiya hoga tu.* I am only a friend,' I said.

'Okay. You can continue chilling in the friendzone and one day, a senior from class 12 will swoop in and steal her from you,' he warned me.

The thought of seeing her with any other guy troubled me a little. Was Saransh right? I looked at Radhika, who was animatedly discussing something with Preeti, the girl who sat in front of her. Jiggy and I weren't her only friends at Pragati anymore. Maybe there were others too. I did spend a lot of time in Veepi's room, away from her.

'I told you so,' Saransh murmured. 'That's what I will say when you come back crying to me,' he added.

'Just shut up, *yaar*,' I said, unconvincingly. Just then, I spotted Ritu Ma'am, our English teacher. I separated from the rest of the class and approached her. I told Saransh I would see him in the class.

'Good morning, ma'am,' I said, with the widest smile I could manage.

'Yes, Yogesh?'

'Ma'am, I was wondering, why don't we have any poetry summits in our school?' I asked.

'Poetry summit? What do you mean?' she asked.

She knew what I was talking about, but she was just taken aback because the idea had come from me. I didn't blame her as this was the first time I had interacted with her in the school and not about any dog-walking-related conversations. I told her all about the poetry open mic I had seen at the dog cafe and how it was a wonderful opportunity for students to share their honest thoughts.

I had promised Radhika I would not force her to do something she was uncomfortable with and I intended to keep it. Still, I wanted to encourage her to overcome her fear by making her want to stand up on stage and speak publicly. A school poetry summit would be the best way to go about it.

'What a wonderful thought, Yogesh,' she said, pronouncing every word in the crispest way possible. 'You're absolutely right. We must have one summit every year.'

'I totally agree, ma'am.'

'I shall definitely raise this with the Principal in our next weekly meeting,' she said and walked off.

During recess, Radhika and I were loitering around the campus after eating together as usual.

It was unusually windy that day. I spotted a little girl hiding behind a tree and cackling as she saw her friend looking for her. They appeared to be in second or third standard. A group of boys and girls was playing Kho Kho together, and thcy were quite loud. A guy, who was often seen on stage during the assembly, was singing on the canteen stairs and his friends were cheering for him. It was a happy day. A breezy afternoon in Faridabad's summer heat was truly a blessing. And everyone was making the most out of it. So was I, by spending it with the girl I literally hadn't stopped thinking about for the last couple of days.

'Why do you want to be an entrepreneur?' Radhika asked. The breeze played with her hair. I wanted to do the same.

But instead, I questioned her in return, 'Why shouldn't I want to be an entrepreneur?' I was trying to act like my heart was NOT beating faster than ever in her presence.

'No, really. Why do you want to be an entrepreneur? I am just curious. Yesterday, you spoke about the books you've been reading. You only read books about building businesses. I don't know other 16-year-olds who do that. What's the hurry?'

It made me think. I knew exactly when this urge had first come in. It was the day that my father came home after a successful union strike. 'Those filthy rich animals finally know what it's like to lose,' he'd crowed. His strike had shaken the company's finances badly. I had grown up hearing my father curse the owners of the company he worked for, for their wealth and power. The way he spoke about it, he sounded so admirable, believing that greed was evil and wealth was poison and all that. And I'd believed it too and hated the businessmen, just like he did. Until I witnessed all the fights between my parents over money.

'I haven't bought a sari in three years,' I remembered my mother saying on one occasion. In class 3, I couldn't read the last few chapters in my secondhand Maths book because the pages were torn and my father didn't have the money to buy a new one. When I brought Sheru home, my mother had worried about the expense and what my father would say, despite her own love for dogs. And then I slowly realised that my father did not lead these strikes because he didn't care for money, but because he didn't want anyone else to have what he didn't. It wasn't grand ideas of freedom and equality that drove him on, but jealousy, pure and simple.

Radhika and I were close, but I couldn't share these things with her yet. I thought of other reasons. And then I remembered. 'I still remember the day I had made some money on my own for the first time. I was in class 7th and I had taken Math tuition for a boy in class 3. He stayed in our neighbourhood and our mothers were quite pally. So, my mom insisted on having me help him. When he not only passed but also scored well in his exams, his mother happily gave me 500 rupees. I had earned it with my own hard work. Looking at that gave me a high,' I narrated.

'So that high made you want to be a businessman?'

'The realisation didn't come to me overnight. But I had learned that having your own money in your pocket brings a lot of comfort - the comfort I didn't have growing up. I've seen my father struggle, I've seen my mother cry. I never wanted to feel that way myself. I know you judge me for making everything about money, but I really like the power it gives,' I smiled.

'When you put it like that… yeah, I suppose that is true. People always want stability and comfort in life, and money gives you that.'

I could never really pinpoint what it was about Radhika that always induced my verbal diarrhoea and made me blurt out things with so much ease about topics I seldom spoke about. But there was definitely *something* about her that brought out a different side of me. I never wanted to lose this version of me. I didn't want to be her *buddy bhaiya*.

'Did you read the book?'

'I think you already know the answer to that,' she smiled.

'Narendra Uncle is very passionate about books and quite well-connected with other libraries and bookstores. When I found out about your admiration for Emily Bee, I reached out to him for help.'

'So it was all planned in advance?'

'I had plans to give you the book someday. But taking you there yesterday was an impulsive decision. When you got upset during the Open Mic, I wanted to do something to cheer you up,' I said.

'That was the sweetest thing anyone's ever done for me. I'll never forget it,' she grabbed my hand and squeezed it lightly.

The moment she touched me, I felt the same giddiness that I had experienced the previous evening. I looked at her fingers around my wrist and continued looking at her soft, pretty hand. She was precious to me. From the way she was holding my hand, it felt like maybe I was to her too. At that very moment, I decided I was going to tell her. Soon. When the time is right.

The bell rang and we went back to class.

'Listen?' I asked her after the last period.

'Yes?'

'Your watermelon mint juice is still pending. Let's go to Goyal's?'

'Actually, it's my dad's birthday today. So we are going out for dinner with Jiggy's family,' she said.

'Oh, happy birthday to uncle then,' I said with a happy face, trying to hide my disappointment.

'He hasn't really liked celebrating his birthdays ever since mom left four years ago,' she shared.

'Can I ask you something?' I asked, after toying with the thought for a moment.

'Why did my mom leave us? I don't really know the actual reason. I just vaguely remember my parents fighting all the time. My father got my custody for some reason and my mom never visited. She calls sometimes, but I mostly try to avoid the calls.'

It was on the tip of my tongue to ask her how she didn't still know about why her father got custody. I realised that she probably just didn't want to tell me and I decided not to push her more.

She looked like she was going to tear up and this time, I reached out and held her hand. The tips of my fingers felt weirdly tingly when I touched her. My heart was pounding and my mouth felt dry. I gulped. I had never felt like that for anyone before. In just a few days, Radhika had become extremely important to me. I knew then that I was falling for her. Big time. I couldn't help but wonder if she felt like that for me too. But she was holding onto my hand, and at that moment, it was enough for me. Her skin was warm and soft and I wanted to never let go.

I had to, after a few minutes as she left with Jigyaasu. That evening was greyer than usual. I realised that I was missing her.

17

My thoughts had now been monopolised by Radhika. I couldn't get myself to concentrate on anything else. I skipped lunch and couldn't get myself to eat dinner either. I went through my texts with Radhika and read through the first one she had sent, a poem about Sheru. It made me smile. I was never active on Instagram and had barely posted one photo of Sheru, but I logged in after a long time that night.

I searched for Radhika Sablok. There were multiple profiles that showed up with that name. But even that tiny circular display picture was enough for me to recognise the girl I was looking for. *My girl* - or at least that's what I wanted her to be. Turned out she didn't post often either and had only twelve photos on her feed. Three of them were her childhood photos with Jigyaasu, she had posted them each to wish him on his birthday in different years. One was a pic of a plate of pasta. 'I don't like the colour pink, but I like it on my pasta.' It didn't make much sense to me as the colour of the pasta definitely wasn't pink.

When I scrolled down and saw the third photo, I couldn't stop staring. It was a simple photo of Radhika standing on the road, wearing a dark blue dress. Her arm was looped with another girl with short hair and a pleasing smile. It was the first time I had seen her in anything other than school uniform or PJs. She looked too pretty. The urge to kiss her came crawling back and every fibre of my being wanted to hold her and do so.

My phone pinged and it was a message from Radhika. It was a sign from the Universe.

'At least follow me first.'

Shit. I had liked one of her photos while scrolling.

'Yes, I was just going to do that. Nice pics,' I messaged.

'Thank you. What are you doing?'

'Just chilling at home,' I replied.

'When are you calling me home?'

When she asked me this, I suddenly looked at my home with a new set of eyes. What would she say on seeing it? It might have seemed congested, but it was neat as well. There was often some residual smell of phenyl. I had never seen any other house with a cloth table, except my own. We had a perforated white one.

'Probably never,' I replied.

'Whyyyyy?' she replied.

While I thought of what to reply to her, she sent another text. 'Achcha, gotta go. Guests are still at home. Good night,' she went offline.

When she left the chat, I got the same sinking feeling I had experienced that day when she had left from school. Our time apart was getting more and more unbearable for me. I decided I was going to tell her. Obviously, it couldn't be in school or Goyal's or some random place. I needed to do it right.

'Just take her to an expensive restaurant, *yaar,*' Saransh said.

We were talking about where I should confess my love to Radhika. I couldn't believe that he was the person whose advice I was seeking. But the truth was that I had no idea how to do such a thing. It was the third period of the day and the teacher hadn't shown up. Radhika and Jigyaasu were not in their seats, which allowed us to discuss freely. The class was mostly quiet, with everyone talking softly among themselves.

'I'm not sure,' I said.

'But what happened to all your rules about not dating and all that? Don't lose focus from the larger picture, *bhai*.'

'That's the thing. What if there's NO larger picture without her? I got the idea for Doggles while talking to her, I made my first prototype with sunglasses she got for me. What if she's the push I needed all my life to truly grow?' I said.

Gupta sir walked in. 'Silence,' he said even before he sat down, looking directly at us. 'Your teacher is absent, so continue with your studies.'

Saransh bent his head over his text and I scribbled some gibberish on my notebook.

'Umm, who are you and what did you do to my friend Yogesh?' he continued in an undertone.

'No, man, seriously. She gives me strength. I couldn't have done the trials without her either. She's been a great support.'

'Oh, *bete*, then *toh* I am here for anything you need. When do you plan to do it?'

That made me hesitate. I actually hadn't thought of any particular time to do this. On an impulse, I said, 'Tomorrow, after school. Can you also bring your brown jacket for me? I had looked very dashing in it when I had worn it for *mamaji*'s wedding.'

'It was a winter wedding. You will suffocate and die if you wear that jacket in this heat,' he said.

'But I wanted to look good for her,' I blurted as I looked at Radhika, who had just entered the class, and admired her cute face.

Stop talking,' Gupta sir said again, louder.

'Sir, we're discussing Physics answers,' Saransh said and lifted his book. In a lower voice, he said to me, 'Wear blue jeans and a white tee with white sneakers. It's a classic combination that can never go wrong.'

'But —'

'No buts. You are Yogesh Mittal! You are making your own money at sixteen and you're soon going to have a million-dollar empire,' he cut me off.

'Billion-dollar empire,' I corrected him.

Any decent restaurant was going to cost money. I did some Math in my mind about how much money I had on me. The truth was that I had a good amount saved up. What added to that was that the next day was payday for my dog walking services. With that amount, I was going to touch forty thousand in my savings, which was the amount I needed to buy my laptop.

'Perhaps, my laptop will have to wait for a few more weeks,' I said.

'Of course. Is there anything more important than Radhika to you?'

'If I'm going to confess to her, it has to be my style,' I said.

'What is your style?'

'That I will take her with me to buy the

laptop. I will make her a part of the most joyful moment of my life. And as we will unpack it, I will confess my love to her.'

'Pick that up!' Jigyaasu yelled.

Radhika and I exchanged a glance and she prodded the class 5 student forward. 'Go on, pick it up,' she said. The kid rolled his eyes but did as he was told. 'You really didn't have to join me for this,' she added. Which was true.

Jigyaasu had gone to the staff room to continue his quest of flattering the teachers and overheard Gajendra Mishra complaining about how hard it was to oversee all the class 5 students, who had to do some campus clean-up drive for the Swachh Bharat campaign. He immediately jumped in and offered to assist in overseeing the juniors. Apparently, the students were too many even for him to handle. Mishra sir asked him to take two friends along to help and he only had one in our class. So, Jigyaasu grudgingly asked me.

'I know there must be some really important Doggles-related task, which is very urgent for you,' she went on.

'I can take a break,' I said. I could not let her know that at the moment, my focus was on something else entirely and all I wanted was to be with her. 'Besides, I need to decide what our next step should be.'

We walked together on the ground, passing students in pairs or trios, and holding bags to drop plastic waste. Jigyaasu had given us a bag to share, too, but so far the only contribution to it was from Radhika's side. 'Do you have any ideas?' she said, as she leaned down to pick up a small *Appy* bottle.

'I think it's time we got a website.'

'Really? That sounds fun,' she said.

'I need to collect some ideas first and go through our research from Veepi's desktop.' Thinking about the desktop made me remember how I had planned to ask her to accompany me to buy my new laptop tomorrow and confess my feelings for her.

'What would you put on the website, anyway?'

'To be honest, I have no idea. Do you?' I asked.

'I think we can clearly see that people react much better when you show them the product instead of describing it to them. The site should have as many pictures as possible.'

She was right. 'We should have taken some yesterday at the dog cafe,' I said.

'Yeah, but for a website, we need much better quality pictures.'

But better pictures were going to need money and after buying my laptop, I would have to begin from ground zero to collect enough money to hire a studio or photographer. For a moment, there was no sound but Jigyaasu scolding some juniors for not working hard enough. He looked at us from across the field, as if ordering us to get a move on. I dragged my feet in response and he turned away with a roll of his eyes.

'I could help,' she offered. 'I have a family friend in Shalimar Bagh who owns a studio. He'll definitely help me out. I think he's even handled a few pet shoots for some owners.'

'Alright,' I said enthusiastically and jumped forward to grab a paper plate that kept fluttering away from Radhika's grasp. I threw it in.

I pressed my lips together, afraid that I would have given too much away by the way I was looking at her and that now she'd suspect what I wanted to do. Of all the ways to confess one's feelings, a campus clean-up drive was definitely the least romantic. But she tossed her head back and said, 'I know, *yaar*. But I've read that Emily Bee book over three times now, so I think we're even.'

I couldn't imagine reading a poetry book twice, let alone three times. But her pleased expression, probably as she remembered some line she had read recently, made me happy as well. As we dumped our load into a trashcan, I said, 'I have something planned tomorrow. Will you come with me after school?'

She looked curiously at me. 'Did you find another library or something?'

'No,' I laughed. 'This is a special occasion for me, but I want you to be a part of it.' I had never talked about these plans to anyone but Saransh. Even my parents did not know how much I had saved up with my dog walking and the little profit from BookMyTijori. It felt right, revealing this to my closest friend, who had stayed by my side for so long. 'I knew I'd eventually need to have a computer of my own to pursue my business ideas and plans, I couldn't exactly run to Veepi's desktop every time I wanted to search something up. So I've been saving up to buy a laptop and I'm going to buy one tomorrow.'

She shrieked and pulled off her glove so she could pat me on the back. 'Yogesh, that's wonderful! Of course, I'll come with you.'

Seeing her delight, I smiled back, but I couldn't help but hope that I would get the same exact smile tomorrow, after I told her my feelings.

18

'Oh, I really needed that,' Radhika said and cracked her back. 'Nothing tastes better than *golgappe* after school hours.'

We were walking back after the clean-up drive and by instinct we'd stopped together at the first roadside vendor selling *golgappes.* We took turns to drag my cycle as we headed toward our usual spot in Fountain Park. Radhika had suggested looking for some good spots for the photoshoot as well.

After we reached the park, I went to pick up Sheru, who joyfully came over to Radhika and rested his head on her lap. I never thought I would feel jealous of Sheru, but here we were. The sun had set already. Everything about this moment was perfect. The hues of orange made Radhika look even more gorgeous. Plus, seeing her with Sheru always made me emotional. I didn't take out my phone. But I captured that moment in my mind.

The sun had almost set. I noticed a girl who was clicking a picture of the sky, which had turned a vivid shade of orange. Somehow, it was only when I saw her that I realised how pretty the sunset looked. What is it about our fascination with sunsets and the sky? The chaotic shapes in the sky and the drop in temperature had a calming effect on me. The three of us sat in silence for a while.

Watching the darkness fall and the lights going on in the street, I realised that I had spent a full day with Radhika, at school and after. If I had spent that much time with Saransh, I'd be tired of him. But I could never get enough of her. She suddenly lay down and said, 'Look at the stars.'

I hadn't realised it was dark already.

I lay down next to her and looked up.

'You know, as a kid, I loved watching space movies. My mom had even gifted me an astronaut costume once, I had won the first prize for fancy dress,' she remembered.

I realised she had no stage fright as a child as she had not only participated in a fancy dress competition but also won it. I looked at her and from her expressions, it looked like she was in pain. Maybe mentioning her mother had brought back some memories. I tried to quickly change the topic.

'You know, when astronauts go to space, one of the first things they notice is how tiny and insignificant the earth is in this gigantic universe. Astronauts have this intense emotional experience when they see first-hand the reality of the earth, so small, such a fragile ball of life, hanging in the void, shielded and nourished by a paper-thin atmosphere,' I said.

'Yeah,' she said, without taking her eyes off the sky.

'It's surreal how from space, all the national boundaries vanish, the conflicts that divide people become less important, we all look like just one big mass of people, fighting our daily battles, without thinking about how inconsequential we are in the bigger scheme of things,' I added.

I knew I was only blabbering random stuff, but I hoped it had changed her mood. She looked at me and smiled and I knew I had.

'True,' she agreed. 'We are also so

insignificant, right? We are just tiny specks on a planet which is itself a tiny speck in the universe. And yet, each one of us thinks we are the most important person in the world. Each one of us thinks we are the centre of the universe. We believe that everyone else is thinking about us, judging us or getting impressed with what we're doing. When the reality is that most people are just too busy worrying about themselves and what we are thinking of them.'

She continued staring at the sky. And I continued staring at her. Radhika was lying next to me and all I wanted to do was reach out and pull her closer. I was breathing deeply. 'Tomorrow,' I thought to myself. I had yet to ask her about the dinner.

We started walking in no direction in particular. My home was around a kilometre from the park and Radhika lived around three kilometres. But I don't think either of us had a destination in mind, as we walked on the streets of Faridabad. Our energy was mellow, in contrast with Sheru, who hadn't tired from all the playing at all.

'You know why I loved the astronaut costume?' she asked, suddenly breaking the silence.

'Why?' I asked.

'Because it made me feel like I could see the world, but the world couldn't see me. The sound of my breath suppressed the noise of the surroundings. It felt like my safe space,' her voice had turned shaky.

Even in sadness, she looked stunning. It was hard for me not to hold her and comfort her.

'When my mom left, she took my safe space with her. I am not talking about the costume, in general. I hate that she never bothered to look back and visit me. She's in Mumbai now. She probably has many friends there. It's like she has found her own world there, and totally forgotten about us,' she said, controlling her tears.

She looked so fragile at that moment, almost like she'd break. I wished I could keep her in my pocket and protect her forever.

'You said, she still calls you. Maybe she misses you as much as you miss her. Maybe she can't visit because she didn't get your custody,' I said.

'Why didn't she fight for me then?'

I didn't know what was the right thing to say in response to that. So we walked without saying anything for a while. Sheru saw a cat on the other side of the road and started barking.

'Do you want to have ice cream?' I asked as I spotted an ice cream cart on the road.

'Yes, but it's my treat,' she said and I didn't fight her.

We sat down on the pavement. It wasn't the cleanest and I didn't expect Radhika to be okay with it, but she was. We had got two choco bars and ate them as the world passed us by on the road. A lady walked up to us, who was holding a bunch of colourful balloons. I paid her 5 rupees and got a yellow one, matching Radhika's bag.

'Here, this is your safe space,' I said, holding out the balloon towards her. As she reached out to take it from me, I let it go. She looked startled. The balloon started floating above us and eventually, it vanished. We had finished eating our ice creams by then.

'Why would you do that?' she demanded an answer.

'That yellow balloon is still your safe space. Just because you can't see it or touch it, doesn't mean your safe space doesn't exist. With or without the astronaut costume, you need to learn to tune out the world and live for just yourself,' I said.

She didn't speak for a moment and kept staring at me. I panicked, wondering if I'd said it all wrong. 'How do you always manage to do this?' she asked.

'Do what?'

'Say the right things, cheer me up, make me feel better about myself.'

'You do the same for me too, you know,' I said. I wondered if I shouldn't wait for the next day and confess my feelings right there. It was evident that we both were in love with each other. I needed her as much as she needed me. We were not in the mall, in the electronics shop, like I had planned. There was a faint smell of cow dung coming from somewhere instead of the usual smells of a mall. Instead of light jazz music, there were occasional horn sounds. Instead of a polite salesman at our service, we were being disturbed by street hawkers every few seconds. But I just knew the moment was right. It was time I told her.

'Ra—' I started speaking.

But she cut me off and said, 'I am glad I found you, Yogi,' she smiled and added, 'Talking to you is so easy. You bring out a side of me that even Gagan doesn't. With you, the words just naturally come out of my mouth. I always end up oversharing. But I don't mind it. I feel so light whenever I share things with you.'

'Gagan?'

'Oh, yes, Gagan and I met in my previous school, Nagpal Public School. We had been close friends since the beginning and then, we started dating last year.'

'You're seeing someone?'

'Yeah,' she said, having no clue about the shock I had just felt.

As she went on about how scared she was about changing schools and how relieved she was to find me, it was as if my whole life was flashing in front of me. My mom had never hit me, but my dad had slapped me twice in my life. For some reason, her words hurt me more than those slaps too. I felt like someone had punched me in the gut. I had read it all wrong. She only saw a friend in me. But I mistook her friendship for something else. The hugs, the hand-holding, lying under the stars - everything was platonic for her. I felt stupid to have romanticised everything in my head.

I realised she was looking at me for a response.

'Why didn't you tell me about Gagan before?' I managed to say, trying hard to sound like a concerned friend.

'I am so sorry, Yogi. You know me, *na*. I take time to open up about things. Somehow the topic never came up. Just never ended up mentioning anything,' she said.

'It's okay. *Chalo*, I am happy for you. I am glad you have someone who loves you because you deserve to be loved,' I asserted.

She smiled. I managed to smile back.

'*Achcha*, now, I'll have to take your leave as I have to take Sheru to the vet. We have an appointment,' I lied.

It was dark and I didn't want to leave her alone. So, I waited till Jiggy came to pick her up. The wait was slightly awkward and mostly silent. But I pretended to be doing something important on my phone and put up a strong front.

But as soon as we said goodbye and I turned my back towards her, I felt a pang of pain. I was absolutely devastated. While walking in haste, I kicked a rock by mistake and hurt my right toe. It hurt like a bitch.

I remembered the poem she had written after meeting Sheru. I remembered our walks during every recess. I remembered our scooty ride. I remembered how we had held hands and ran from the market. It all felt like a dream now. I felt embarrassed.

As I walked, I felt like I had stepped on something. I lifted my foot to see that I had squished a cockroach. There had been no sound but just a sinking feeling of having stepped on something. A 3D organism had been flattened to 2D in a matter of microseconds. I wondered if it had seen it coming in the dark and tried to run for its life. Or it had just been chilling one moment and the very next moment, plop.

I continued to walk, with a crime scene on my shoe. Death being splattered with every step that I took. I felt sorry for the cockroach for a second, but then the very next moment I could relate to it. If anyone knew what it felt like to be squished into a thousand pieces at that moment, it was me. I had had my own shell cracked and had my guts spewed all over just a few minutes ago. My insides had been exposed.

The cockroach is a cocky organism. It takes pride in being a survivor. For millennia it has survived multiple extinction events with almost no evolution. I hadn't been very different. I took pride in surviving some difficult events myself. But this. The cockroach and I, both had been hit by things we didn't know how to handle: our arrogance, knocked out of us in a moment. But I walked on, alive, unlike the cockroach.

I reached my cycle and I just looked at it. I looked at its awkward black paint and stickers, which I had designed himself. Suddenly, the same cycle felt really ugly. Why would any girl want to be with a guy with a cycle? Where would she even sit? On the rod in front of him or the carrier at the back. As I rode the cycle home, I had one of those moments that I had every now and then: when I told myself that I was going to be very very rich in life. I knew that Radhika was the last person who cared about money or what vehicle I used. But still, I couldn't help these feelings, as I sweated heavily.

On my way home, my eyes fell on Unity One Mall. I tapped my pocket and realised that I had the cash with me. I walked in and bought the laptop all by myself. What should have been the happiest moment of my life felt like just another one. Somehow, this victory felt hollow.

'Sir, do you want to keep the laptop in your bag?' the shopkeeper asked me.

I nodded but realised that I had some prototypes of Doggles in my bag, which left very little space. I took the Doggles in my hand and smashed them on the ground. Everybody at the laptop shop looked at me. I then stomped all over them with my feet, as the shopkeeper looked in horror.

'Sir?' he said, almost pleading with me to stop. I was not the kind of person who gave in to such impulses, but I had never been so dejected either.

I came out of the store and a little boy came up to me, trying to sell peanuts. Usually, I would have been impressed by his hustle. But right now, I wanted to tell him to quit.

'I don't think I ever want to go back to entrepreneurship ever again,' I declared, more to myself than anyone else.

When I reached home, I was relieved to see that my father was not back home yet. I had no energy to listen to his taunts or fight him that night. In fact, I had no energy left to do anything at all. I told Maa I had already eaten outside and threw myself on the bed. I kept staring blankly at the ceiling, hoping for that strong pang of pain to pass. But it didn't.

When I couldn't sleep, I decided to unpack my laptop. I turned on the hotspot on my phone and as if to have an auspicious start to my new machine, the first thing I played was an episode of 'My First Million' podcast.

My phone pinged after a while and it was a message from Saransh. 'How did it go with *bhabhi*?' I read the text notification. I kept my phone aside and tried to sleep. But I couldn't. I remembered I had taken my school bag to the park that evening to carry the prototypes and the photoshoot plans, which Radhika had sketched on some sheets of paper. I looked at the plans. She had used her hat and different things she owned as props in the plan. It was all her. I felt guilty for mistaking her friendship and support as something else altogether.

I got out of bed and took the drawings out and replaced them with some books and a few notebooks that were required for the next day's classes. I kept the drawings in the cupboard and carefully covered them with some of my T-shirts. The last thing I wanted was for mom or dad to find them.

My phone buzzed again and it was Saransh. 'Let's not talk about this for some time?' I replied to him.

'What happened? Is everything okay?' he replied. But I didn't respond. My phone pinged a few more times, but I didn't bother to check. I eventually drifted off to sleep at some point.

19

I resolved that I would be more *normal* from now on. By normal, I meant doing activities which guys my age are expected to do. That evening, after several months, I went to play cricket in the nearby park. After cricket, I hung out with the neighbourhood boys and tried my best to be able to relate to their struggles in life.

I spent the next few days in autopilot mode. Whenever my brain would start thinking of some business idea, I would nip it in the bud itself. For the first time, I started thinking about going to college. I began to pay attention in class and started looking up engineering colleges.

If I was serious about joining an engineering college, I would have to join some coaching class. There was no way I could afford to pay the amount that was required for these. The only option I had was to sell my laptop.

That would generate enough money to cover at least a year's fee for a good coaching institute. Did I really need this laptop now?

I didn't go to the Physics Lab for two days. On the third day, my class had a period in the Physics Lab and I couldn't avoid a visit. After the class, I saw Veepi and told him to dismantle his laboratory. I didn't want to experiment anymore.

I tried hard to look over Gajendra Mishra's idiosyncrasies and focus on what was being taught. I really wanted to discontinue the dog walking thing as well, but I needed the money. But apart from that, I was not going to do or think anything related to entrepreneurship. Focusing on what was being taught made sure my brain had no downtime to think of random ideas.

I realised that nothing made me happier than playing cricket with my friends from my neighbourhood. They played with tennis balls and were under constant stress of breaking some glass in some houses. When I was playing, I didn't think about anything else. It was like meditation, as all of my thoughts were just focused on the game. The after-feel of endorphins was just a bonus.

Saransh stayed by me during this time. When I told him that Radhika was seeing someone, a part of me thought he would take it jokingly. I imagined him saying, 'Don't be such a Devdas, yaar,' and mocking me for being sad for a girl. But I guess even clowns have hearts. What he said instead was, 'How is Doggles doing?'

'I don't feel like working on them anymore,' I said. I could not bring myself to say that I had broken the prototypes we'd made.

'Don't tell me it's because of Radhika,' he said, shocked.

'Only a little,' I said defensively. 'She did help me a lot with my idea for Doggles. But I don't think I can work with her anymore. Anyway, I'm not sure if it's a good idea in the first place. She inspired me to pursue it, she planned the photoshoot and helped with the prototypes. I can't go back to it without her.'

'It was your idea in the first place,' he said. 'And you were managing just fine without her. Come on, *yaar.* You've known this girl for less than a month, but you've been dreaming about entrepreneurship for ages.' For the first time, he said that word through to the end, correctly. 'Don't give up now.'

His message was clear. It was time to focus on the business. I was back to being the old Yogesh Mittal. Yes, I was still hurting. But I didn't have any time to waste in sulking. I couldn't find fault with his advice, but I just nodded.

'Who is she dating?' was the only question he asked about Radhika.

'Someone named Gagan in her previous school,' I said.

'I'm just relieved there is nothing between her and that Jigyaasu.'

'Of course, there is not.'

'But anyway, welcome to the friendzone, brother. I am the mayor of this place,' he laughed. He was doing what he knew best - using his humour to make me feel better. I guessed he was also feeling guilty for encouraging me when it came to my feelings for Radhika.

I smiled.

Soon Gajju sir came in and started his class. I spent most of the lectures looking outside the window and gazing at nothing in particular. It was the first time I was nursing a broken heart. Had someone warned me about how painful it was going to be, I would have actively steered clear of the L word.

The moment our fourth period was over, I vanished from the classroom and found refuge in Veepi's room. I was scared. What if I hung out with Radhika and she started telling me stories of how amazing Gagan was? No way. I tried to be a good person, but I didn't have it in me to hear that. It had taken a toll to allow myself to fall for someone in the first place. I had nothing against her. But I needed to keep a distance from her as the pain was unbearable. I needed to do that for Doggles. And for my sanity.

I used Veepi's computer and started reading about website building. I had requested Saransh to lock the door from the outside and open it only when recess was over. I didn't want to be found. By Radhika. I convinced myself that I had shunned her from my thoughts. But just then, there was a knock on the door. There was a split second in which I turned around to see who it was. In that second, I became aware of how badly my heart was hoping it was her. I just wished it was her smiling face waiting for me. I just needed to have her next to me through this.

But it was Saransh. The moment our eyes met, I knew that he knew what I was feeling.

As the final period's bell rang, I almost sprinted out of the room. It had been hard enough to not make eye contact with her throughout the day. Starting from the first period, I had run into trouble when the Chemistry teacher took us to the lab and asked us to pair up. Radhika had turned to me so casually, as though she was sure I would be her partner. I had felt guilty, but not enough to overcome every muscle in my body that made me stay away. I had paired with Saransh instead and she had gone dejectedly to Jiygaasu, but he'd already paired up. It turned out we were an odd number and so she ended up in a corner all by herself. Throughout the day, she turned around every chance she could get to talk to me, but I refused to make eye contact.

After she was caught in the act by one of the teachers and scolded for it, she stopped.

I knew she was waiting for the bell to ring and I had already packed up my bag, intending to make a run for the door that would put Usain Bolt to shame. But it was too late, for the other students had already crammed up near the door and I couldn't pretend I didn't hear her when she called out my name.

'Are you okay?' she said.

'Yeah, everything is fine,' I replied, quite aware that I was a terrible liar.

'Why are you acting like this?' A few girls jostled past her and their elbows hit her shoulder. It must surely have hurt, but she did not stop staring at me.

I could not ignore the hurt so clear in her wide eyes. 'I'm sorry, I have something important regarding Doggles. I have to rush,' I said and began to leave. My heart was racing, but this was the only way I could stop it from bursting out of my chest.

'Where are you going?'

'Veepi is waiting for me,' I said.

The hurt shifted to something like

stubbornness. 'Fine, then, I'll also come with you. I haven't seen Veepi in a while.'

'No, you can't!' By now, the class was nearly empty, and my loud voice resonated through the room. Radhika's jaw slipped open and she didn't say anything for a moment. Trying to maintain a calm tone, I said, 'I meant that I'm going somewhere you can't come. It'd be awkward if you do.' I wasn't lying. Veepi was waiting for me. I had told him during recess that I would come with him to the hardware shop that he owned.

'Fine, then…' She tugged at her bag straps absently. 'How about after?'

'No, no, I have to work on my Doggles website.'

'You bought your laptop?'

I stared at her in panic and nodded dumbly. I had completely forgotten that I had told her to join me. She blinked and her confusion was evident. For a moment, I wondered if her social anxiety would start acting up again, but all she said was, 'Yogesh, what's wrong?'

'*Arre*, I just forgot that I had promised to take you along.'

'I never imagined that you'd be like this,' she said. 'What will I do when my own Life Coach treats me this way?'

I had no words to say to that. So, I fled.

I met Veepi in the Physics Lab. He was having lunch alone, with his five-compartment steel tiffin box spread on the table. He flashed his usual toothy smile when he saw me.

'Come, come, Yogi saab,' he said. 'Here, have this *bhaingan ka bharta* made by your *Bhabhi ji.*'

I hadn't had lunch, but I just didn't feel like eating. Veepi was watching me, and so I fired up his desktop. But my mind was blank. I couldn't think of what to type in the Google search button, I didn't know how to build a website and didn't have the energy to research it. I played with the cursor, watching it zigzag across the screen. Never had I imagined I would see myself like this, with full access to the internet and not using it to the best of my ability.

Finally, I knew how my classmates managed

to do it. All that was left for me to truly while away my time was to go to YouTube and watch videos of dancing puppies. But the moment I started allocating space for the pictures, her thoughts came floating back. I fidgeted around with the keyboard, trying to type out a decent product description for Doggles. But I kept spewing basic shit and backspacing over and over again. How was I so bad at describing *my own product*? After half an hour, I was still stuck. Even though Veepi was a successful businessman, who had been a mentor to me, this definitely wasn't something he was going to be able to help with.

And just like that, I found myself missing Radhika even more than before. She would have surely come up with something great very easily. She had a way with words. With her flair for writing, she'd have aced this. From bringing her mom's sunglasses for the prototypes to telling me how to approach people during the trials, from giving me pep talks to planning the most elaborate photoshoot - she had always been a *huge* support. Radhika always had a solution whenever I got stuck and she *always* said the right things. I missed her. I realised not having her in my life sucked both for myself and Doggles.

After wasting some more time and not managing to write anything decent, I took a few printouts of the photoshoot plans. Veepi was done with his work and it was time for us to leave.

'You sure you want to come with me to my boring shop?' he asked.

I nodded affirmatively. I could have done anything to not be left with my thoughts. I just wanted to talk about business with someone and Veepi was my most aware friend. Veepi's hardware store was a few kilometres away from school in Naharpur Village. When I was in class 9, I had once visited that area for an errand. I had spotted his familiar face at a shop called 'Ved Prakash Hardware Store'. When I greeted him and he found out I was from Pragati, he looked like he had seen a ghost. I later found out that school employees weren't allowed to work elsewhere. It had been our little secret since then.

As we walked towards the parking lot, I asked him how his business was doing. Even as he responded, I felt a rush of comfort at being with him. Anyone else would've gotten annoyed or asked me to mind my business. But Veepi always indulged me and my curiosity. He was an entrepreneur after all. And he understood my hunger to know more. Veepi *bhaiya* was my only entrepreneur friend.

'What happened?' Veepi asked as we walked on a little more. 'Your female friend didn't come today?'

20

When I got home, I found several messages from Radhika waiting for me on my phone.

'What's happening, Yogesh?'

'Are you alright?'

'Is there something you aren't telling me?'

'Hellooo???'

I could block all her questions, but one of them was particularly pinching me. Even if I could shun her as a friend, I couldn't as her Life Coach. I didn't want her to feel like I had alienated her. Because of her mother, she already had abandonment issues. I didn't want to be *that friend* who abandoned her after taking all the help he could for his business idea. That's not good behaviour for a Life Coach or even a friend. Suddenly, I felt terrible about avoiding her all day.

'Hey, Radhika. All is well. I am sorry, I was

a little caught up with Doggle-related stuff. I'll see you tomorrow at school?' I replied.

'But what happened?! I've been so worried? Why are you acting like this?' she sent.

'Just generally stressed about a few things,' I replied.

'There is nothing that we can't handle together,' she replied.

I didn't have it in me to reply to that. The word 'together' stuck out for me. That was the whole problem. There was no 'together' between us.

The phone lit up–she was calling me. I couldn't exactly let it ring forever, and besides I knew she would just keep calling me.

'Hello,' I said.

'Finally!' she sounded even more annoyed than I felt, which was an incredible achievement. 'I've been texting, what's the matter with you?'

'Nothing,' I said. Such a lame answer.

'Nothing,' she repeated, mockingly. 'Did you work on Doggles? I thought we could do a few more trials tomorrow, see if more people want to wear them.'

My heart sank into my stomach. How could I possibly tell her that I'd broken them in my fit of rage?

'Yogesh?' she said again. Then she snapped, '*Yaar*, you've never shut up once in all the time I've known you, don't start now.'

'I broke them,' I said, angered by her insult. 'A few days ago.'

There was silence from the other end. I held the phone away from my ear for the inevitable.

'What? On purpose? What for?' I could hardly tell the truth. But she took my silence as some sort of answer anyway. 'Yogesh, I know you came up with the idea for Doggles, but don't forget that I have worked just as hard as you have on this. If you thought it was a bad idea, why didn't you simply say so?'

She was right about that part, at least. When I broke the Doggles, I'd completely forgotten that they belonged to her as well. She had literally brought some of her mother's last belongings with her. 'I'm sorry,' I said sincerely. 'I've never had a friend help me with my ideas. I completely forgot.'

'Achha, it's okay,' she said and I could feel that she was trying to pacify me. 'We'll try again tomorrow. Or someday.'

I stood there in silence, long after the call was cut. Someday, indeed. I didn't know when I would ever feel alright enough to look her in the face and pretend I was just fine. But nor could I continue like this forever. My train of thought was disturbed by a sound from the living room. *'Namak mehenga ho gaya hai kya?'* Dad shouted. He must be upset about the amount of salt in his *dal.*

I felt suffocated. I needed some silence, not only from these external voices but also from the sounds inside my head. Hearing his voice made me feel utterly alone. So, I did what I usually did when I needed some time to myself.

I grabbed Sheru from our verandah and left for a walk. I put on an episode of My First Million podcast and walked briskly in no direction in particular. By the time my legs began to feel tired, I had finally managed to slow down my mental replay of my phone call with Radhika. I looked at my phone and clicked on the list of contacts. I wanted to call her again. But she loved someone else.

When I came back after my short walk, there was something heavy about the atmosphere of the living room. 'Come, sit here,' my father ordered sternly as soon as I entered. He was sitting on the sofa, with his bottle of cheap whisky open. The TV was on. Aaj Tak was covering a piece of news about communal disharmony.

As Dad saw my eyes wandering towards the television set, he reached out for the remote and switched it off. There was an eerie silence in the room. I noticed my mom was hiding behind the door curtains. She always made sure she was around in case things got serious and I needed any rescue.

I knew disobeying my father when he was drinking wasn't exactly a good idea. So, I took a seat.

'What have you been up to?' he asked with a straight face.

'Class 11 is as challenging as everybody says,'

I said. 'Chemistry is giving me a tough time.'

'Hmm, study hard and it won't be that difficult.' He was making another drink for himself. 'What else have you been doing apart from studying?'

'Nothing much. Enjoying cricket in the morning and spending some time with friends,' I said.

'That's nice, what else have you been doing?' he probed further.

The realisation struck me at that moment. Did he know about Doggles? Why else would he be asking me all these questions? But I had been so careful about keeping it all a secret. How could he possibly know?

And just then, my eyes fell on something under the centre table. These were the printouts I had taken at Veepi's. SHIT. I had taken them out of the bag and kept them in the cupboard when I returned home after buying my laptop. I must've forgotten them there. How could I be so stupid?

'I've been trying different ways of making money, like I always do. I'm currently working on this –'

'This is what you've been working on!' he shouted. I was stopped mid-sentence by my father, as he pulled out all the sheets of paper and waved them in my face.

I looked at my mom and she didn't make eye contact with me. I realised what must have happened. *Maa* must've found the sheets in the cupboard while cleaning it and thought they belonged to my father. Maybe she mistook them for something Dad had printed for his work at the factory. I felt slightly betrayed, but I knew it wasn't her fault.

It had been many days since we'd talked about my dreams of starting a business. I'd imagined so many counters, so many comebacks, to each of his arguments. My Dad couldn't have picked a worse time to talk about this though. The last thing I wanted was to defend my dreams.

'I work all day, all night for you. And you think you will be a *nawaab* if you make these *kutte ke chashme*?' Dad said while pointing at the photoshoot plans.

But his sneering voice egged me on. '*Haan, papa*. I truly think I will be. Why can't you let me try? If I fail, that's on me too. I know you can't feel proud or be supportive like any other dad. But at least don't diss my idea,' I replied.

'Why are you in such a hurry to be rich, *beta*?' His tone was much softer. 'The faster the money comes, the faster it leaves.'

'I'm almost seventeen. Soon, I will be an adult. I can dream about my entrepreneurial journey and earning now, don't you think?'

'You want to be like one of those, one of the people I fight every day?' I had grown up hearing about *those people.* They were my father's bosses, the people he was always fighting against, as the union leader in his factory. Over the years, my father had become so bitter towards them that he had started hating anyone who was doing better than us in life. He would come back home after a strike, crowing about all the rich people he'd defeated, making it out to be some kind of superhero tale. But the next week, he'd simply gone right back to work. What kind of victory was that?

'All my life,' I said, 'all I've ever heard is you arguing with my mother over money. You didn't want me to save Sheru because you'd have to pay for his food, you couldn't buy me a new Math book, so I had to make do with Saransh's book–I never complained about it, either. But I don't want that to be my life as well. I'm trying to make enough to live in comfort, without having to struggle for each tiny luxury. What's wrong with that?'

'Ah, why even talk about this,' he said, and sneered. 'Anyway, you don't have what it takes. You only have big and fancy dreams, not the capability to actually do them well.'

'You told me that same exact thing when I said I would never borrow another paisa from you. But I haven't, have I? You thought I'd come begging, saying sorry, but I never did. I'm not as much of a loser as you are, Dad.'

For a moment, I was sure my dad would hit me. His hand raised, but right then, his phone rang. He turned toward it–one of his bosses was calling. I hurriedly made my escape. I wanted to pick up the photoshoot plans because I was afraid they'd be destroyed by my father. But one needs to pick their battles. I promised myself that I needed to become a billionaire as fast as possible.

21

'*Bhai*, you look like shit. Have you not been eating, sleeping or umm... bathing at all?' Saransh looked at me with pity in his eyes. We were walking towards class after the morning assembly.

'Nothing like that. Just couldn't sleep properly last night because of a power cut in our area,' I lied.

'And what's happening with Doggles?'

'I managed to create a basic website, but I am so lost when it comes to the content. I need to write the product description, about us etc. But I've not managed to come up with anything decent. I have just been backspacing everything.'

'I wish I could help, *yaar*. But you know very well that I suck at writing too,' he said.

I noticed Radhika and Jiggy walking by. She

caught me looking at them and smiled. It would have been awkward if I hadn't, so I smiled back too. It took every ounce of my energy.

The rest of the day is a blur in my mind. It's almost as if I was sleepwalking through it all. A few days ago, I was losing my sleep because I was in love. Then, I was unable to sleep because I was heartbroken. And the night before, I couldn't catch any rest as I was worried my dad would shatter my dreams like I had destroyed the Doggles prototypes. I had also lost my appetite. I never skipped my showers though, I just hadn't shaved in the last three days and maybe that's why I looked a little unkempt. I needed to snap out of the zombie mode.

My mother, in the meantime, had decided that after the whole family drama of yesterday, what I needed was to go to the temple and calm down. I didn't think I could withstand being in a state of tension with my mother in addition to my father, so I went along.

At the steps to the temple, I caught sight of a familiar face. Jigyaasu was apparently as religious as he was nerdy. I didn't want to talk to him again, but right as we moved forward, he turned around. He was initially startled, but then he got a knowing smile on his face. I knew he was aware that Radhika and I were not on the best of terms at the moment. My mother went on ahead into the temple, leaving me to face him.

'Ah, the Founder of Doggles himself,' he said, with obvious sarcasm.

'Ah, the future Head Boy,' I replied, trying to match the sarcasm in his voice.

'Are you still working on that idea or have you realised how silly it is?'

I didn't reply. I wondered how much of the situation between Radhika and me did he understand. On one hand, he had very limited social skills and seemed untouched by any emotional wavelength. On the other hand, there were occasions where he showed great maturity and understanding behaviour. There was an unusual element of repulsion in his voice.

'Thank God, at least Radhika is not wasting any more time on it,' Jigyaasu added.

The very mention of Radhika's name from his mouth infuriated me. I don't know if he did, but I interpreted it as if he was deriving joy from our fight. I felt a surge of anger seep into myself.

'Shut up,' I said. 'What do you know about entrepreneurship? All you know is to flatter teachers and wear the best-ironed tie in the history of the world. Have you ever made friends?'

'At least, I know people don't have friends only for some personal benefit.'

That comment hit me hard. So, Jigyaasu did understand everything. The shock must have shown on my face because I saw a hint of a smile on him, as he watched me squirm. 'First her mother left her and now you,' he said, as a final blow. He did one more pranam and walked off. As people around me walked around with their daily spiritual chores, I felt like a world had shifted within me. The person who had helped me the most and so selflessly was being shut off by me. How could I look at myself in the mirror?

I took a long cold bath at home, ate some *rajma chawal*, played with Sheru for a while and even took an afternoon nap. In the evening, I was finally feeling like myself again. That's when I checked my phone for the first time that day and realised Radhika had sent two lengthy messages - the product description and the content for the 'About Us' section of Doggles.

I thought I couldn't feel worse than I already did for ignoring her, this just added gunpowder to the fire. Here I was, wasting my time in self-pity and she was working on Doggles. This merited a call to her. I tried to assess if I had it in me to hear her voice. What if she said hello and I choked up or something? But the truth was that I just had to call her what she had done.

'Hey, Yogi,' she chirped. I felt a pang of guilt again for trying to distance myself from her.

'Hi. Thank you for the write-ups. But how did you know?' I asked.

'I overheard your conversation with Saransh. And he was right. You did look like shit. I hope you feel better soon,' she sounded concerned.

'I'm better already,' I said. If I couldn't tell her the real truth about why I acted so distant, I could at least give her something close to it. 'My father found the photoshoot plans, actually.'

'Oh, no,' she said, again demonstrating how clearly she understood my problems. 'Is that why you destroyed the Doggles prototypes?'

'Yes. But then I realised that I couldn't let my father get me down and I've been trying to make up for all the time I've lost moping. That's why I couldn't spend much time with you.'

'Haan, that's okay. Look, you're the most focused person I've ever met. And you've helped me so much with my anxiety. Can I return the favour? Can I be your Life Coach now?'

'Sure.'

'Do you know what blue zones are?' she quizzed.

'No, what are they?'

'Blue zones are the parts of the world where people live their longest lives, mostly till 100 years of age. And all of these places have one thing in common. People stay connected with their community. Humans are social beings and we need company to survive and thrive,' Radhika informed me.

'Oh, okay,' I said, a tad confused.

'I am saying all this to you so you know that you don't need to go through it all alone. I am your friend. I am here for you.'

It was impossible to *un-love* a sweetheart like her. I decided to let things go and maintain my friendship with her.

When the idea of the photoshoot first came to my mind, I had imagined placing Sheru in someone's house's living room and just clicking a camera button. It turned out to be a lot more work.

As soon as we walked in with Sheru, the studio owner's jaw dropped in horror. 'Is that the dog?' he asked.

'Yes, why?' Radhika said. I glanced at the rows of pictures on the walls. They were all exotic breeds, perfectly trimmed. Some had bowties and others had colourful outfits on. Compared to them, Sheru did not look at all glamorous.

'I thought you'd have a Cocker Spaniel or something, At least a lab. Who does photoshoots of an indie breed, Radhika?'

I wanted to defend myself, but I held back. This was Radhika's father's friend, so I couldn't exactly step in and anger him. But I also didn't want Radhika to get nervous. I tugged on Sheru's leash, intending to leave.

Radhika did not take a step back, though. 'So what? Is there a rule that only exotic breeds should have beautiful pictures taken of themselves? So many animal activists are promoting the adoption of indie breeds.'

'What if it poops?' he asked.

'Sheru is seven years old. He was potty trained when he was a month old,' I said. I wanted to tell the photographer that even he would have been at least two years old when he stopped pooping his pants but decided against it. 'If you don't want to do it, we can take back our deposit.'

The studio owner softened on hearing this. I let out a sigh of relief, hoping that was the end of it. But the real challenge was something else. Sheru was startled by the lights and started barking. No amount of petting, fussing and treats could settle him down long enough for a shoot. I noticed Radhika shooting nervous glances back at the photographer, who was looking again and again at his watch.

Finally, Radhika turned the direction of the main light so it did not shine directly onto the stool where Sheru sat. This seemed to do the trick, and Sheru sat down for the first time. The photographer brought out a coat to put on Sheru, but it was too big for him.

'Why all this trouble anyway,' the photographer murmured. 'He doesn't look that great anyway.'

I remembered what Jigyaasu had said about Sheru once. *He is not even a good-looking dog.* I tried to shut out all negative thoughts and tried to focus on the job at hand. I had tried to get other dogs as well. I had spoken to the people whose dogs he walks if he could borrow their dogs for a photoshoot. All I got were weird stares, as people wondered if he was serious. Ritu Talwar understood the requirement, but she wasn't comfortable in letting Estella out of her eyes for that long.

'He looks so cute,' Radhika said on seeing him. 'He is going to be a rage on Instagram with these pictures.'

The next challenge was to make Sheru look at the camera for long enough for a picture to be clicked. It was not easy to keep Sheru in one place with the Doggles on. First off, he would never look at the photographer, only at Radhika or me. Radhika decided to take the camera herself and shoot the pictures while I tried to attract his attention. Every time he looked in the camera's direction, Radhika clicked the camera. But by the time the picture was captured, Sheru would have either looked away or got up in excitement, wagging his tail like he thought we were playing with him.

'I'm shooting at the highest possible shutter speed to make sure there is no shake because of his movements, but even that is not helping,' Radhika said. It was only after I started moving the light to get Sheru's attention in the right direction that we could get some pictures.

But there was something not right in the pictures. The photographer had done a good job, but the fact that Sheru was not happy was too evident. It didn't send the right message for Doggles.

'Let's take a *chai* break?' Radhika suggested, after having tried for two hours. The studio owner told us that there was a *chai* shop around two blocks away. As we came out for chai, we noticed that there was a park quite close to the studio. Sheru started pulling me towards the park. I was too tired for any games by now, but Sheru didn't relent, I had to give in and go to the park.

'I think he's trying to tell us something,' Radhika said. 'He is telling us that the park is a much better studio than the studio itself.' She convinced the photographer to lend her the camera for an hour and we left Sheru to run around. After a long time, Sheru seemed genuinely happy, bounding up to us on the lawn. It was easy from then on. Radhika clicked one after the other and we got decent pictures of all of the prototypes. In the natural morning light, against the backdrop of the grass and vibrant-coloured flowers, Sheru looked like a real *sher*.

Again, the thought struck me that I really needed Radhika and her input. But it was more than just that. I simply enjoyed being with her. I felt more at peace than with anyone else in my life when we walked or worked together. Even if I found it uncomfortable, it was still preferable to being alone.

22

I had gotten used to looking at the back of Radhika's head every few minutes. I would wonder what would be going through it. I could tell she was often zoned out during classes. With time, it seemed as if she had no idea what the teacher was saying. I realised I should discuss this with her in our next conversation as her Life Coach. It felt like Gajendra Mishra had realised this as well. Maybe, teachers can sense discomfort in students, just like dogs can sense fear in people.

'So, Radhika Ji, are you going to tell the class where you were in the second period?' the teacher asked, as Radhika finally became focused enough to hear what he was saying. 'I'm told you were bunking that period.'

I watched from the back, as Radhika's shoulders dropped. I could almost see her face shrinking under the rebuke. She had never said a word of complaint to me about all the bunking we'd done together. But I should have known that it would put us in trouble at some point. Still, I knew for sure that Radhika had not bunked that particular period. She'd sat at the same seat as where she was sitting right now.

The whole class had its eyes on her, as she stood, bewildered at the accusation being thrown at her. She opened her mouth, but no words came out. As she seemed to have gone blank, guilt wrapped itself around me. I'd never seen her breaking any other school rule except when she bunked with me. Now, I could guess that it was because she was avoiding this exact situation, where the teacher singled her out in front of the whole class for a scolding.

As Gajendra Mishra spewed a few more angry sentences at her, I tried to figure out what was happening. Why was Gajendra Mishra blatantly lying about something so trivial? I was just about to intervene when he started laughing as loudly as he could.

'It was a joke, a prank, Radhika. I know you didn't bunk the class,' he said, in between laughing. Nobody in the class joined him in his laughter except, of course, Jigyaasu.

Radhika left the class without asking and went to the washroom. The teacher moved on like nothing had happened, but I couldn't keep sitting. I needed to check on her. I made an excuse that I needed to go to the washroom urgently. I think the teacher knew that I was lying, but he let me go anyway. It was easy to see that Radhika needed some help.

I caught a glimpse of Radhika entering the girls' washroom. I walked up to its door and debated with myself, if it was worth the potential trouble to enter. I had just raised my hand to open the door when I heard footsteps; Ritu Talwar ma'am was walking down the hallway. She looked at me in surprise and I pretended to tie up my shoelace.

I waited outside in agony, hoping that Radhika was alright. No other girls walked by, who I could ask to check up on her. I had no other option except to wait. A good fifteen minutes later, she came out with a pale face. She didn't say anything when she saw me but went to the water cooler nearby.

'Hey, are you okay–'

'I don't want to talk about it,' she said. Her

voice sounded so cold that I stood in silence while she washed up.

'Gajendra sir is an idiot,' I said at last. 'Cheer up.'

She ran a hand through her hair to tame some flyaways. 'I'll cheer up better if we talk about something else. Like whether you're free this evening.'

My heart jumped in surprise. She had never asked a question like that. 'Sure,' I said, as calmly as I could while my heart beat so hard it nearly broke my rib cage. 'Why?'

She smiled at me. 'I have a surprise planned for you.'

'Here's your mint watermelon juice,' I said as I took a seat at Goyal's.

'Thanks.'

'So what's the surprise?'

The look of mischief on her face grew. I had asked her that at least a dozen times since we left the school compound. 'Mmmm,' she purred with her eyes closed as she finally took a sip of the beverage she had been wanting to have.

I laughed. 'Arre, come on. We're here, you have your drink, what are we waiting for?'

'The surprise will come,' she said serenely.

'Can you give me a hint?'

'No. You bought your laptop without me,' she said as she stirred her drink with the straw. 'This is payback for that.'

I couldn't fault her for that, so I sat back, gathering up what little of my patience I had.

I noticed she had finished her juice. I had almost finished my lemonade too. 'Do you want anything else?' I asked.

'Yes, I want you to meet someone. Turn around,' Radhika casually instructed me.

As I turned, I noticed a group of four boys sharing a fruit plate and a girl in a school uniform walking into the shop.

'Meet whom?' I asked while taking the last sip of my lemonade.

'Meet Gagan.'

The name Gagan had been throbbing in my

head like a headache, but the idea of seeing the person made my heart sink. I looked at the group of boys and tried to figure out who it was. It couldn't be the really fair guy with cosmetics in his hair. He was just too perfect to be Radhika's style. She liked damage. It couldn't be the chubby guy who seemed too lazy to keep up with the speed at which her thoughts moved. One guy had a cigarette in his hand, which completely ruled him out. That left the fourth guy but elimination.

'Who is it?' I asked.

Radhika pointed at the girl in uniform. I almost spat out my drink. *Oh my God. OH MY GOD.* Gagan was a girl? What? Really? Radhika was gay?

By now, the group had caught sight of Radhika. The girl took her hand out of her pocket in a tiny wave like I'd seen the British royals do on camera. Her face seemed oddly familiar until I realised that I'd seen her before on Radhika's Instagram page, with their arms around each other. At the time, I'd dismissed it, thinking they were merely friends.

I could see more than a few eyes following her as she walked through the restaurant.

Maybe it was her bare midriff and the tight crop top, or the smooth, confident way she moved. She had a tiny smile on her face, like she knew the attention she was attracting, but she did not look at anyone but Radhika.

She stopped beside me, and the smile widened. Up close, I knew she was taller than Radhika. She seemed like she was quite rebellious and feisty - the polar opposite of the sweet and dainty Radhika.

'Hi Yogesh, I've heard a lot about you,' said the short-haired girl. 'Gagandeep Kaur this side,' she added.

'So, let me get this straight. Gagan is a girl?' Saransh almost screamed in the middle of the ground.

I nodded.

I knew I'd find him there as he had stayed back post-school for the *Marampatti* league with a bunch of juniors. When he saw my face, he knew it was an emergency and excused himself from the match. We were walking towards the main gate when I broke the news to him.

After laughing hysterically for a while, he finally paused.

'And she never mentioned it to you, supposedly her new best friend?' he asked.

'*Yaar*, honestly, I have so many questions running through my mind. But there was no appropriate way to ask them,' I said.

'I can imagine, *bhai*,' he tried to sympathise, but I could tell he was still controlling his laughter.

'Stop laughing, *yaar*. I am feeling numb. I don't know how to process this,' I told him.

My heart was already broken. But the moment when she introduced me to Gagan, it felt like someone had run a truck over all the remaining pieces.

'Sorry, man. It's just hard not to. I mean, you finally fell in love for the first time. And that girl turned out to be someone who's also into girls. If Gagan was some bratty NCR boy, I swear I would have picked him in a rucksack and beaten the shit out of him for you. But even that can't be done now,' he said.

My dad not only hated my business idea but

also threatened me to stop working on it. The girl I loved had not only friendzoned me, but she was gay. It seemed as if just like Saransh, even life was making a mockery of me.

I was happy for Radhika, I truly was. Gagan seemed like a great girl. But how would you feel if you finally decided to let go and freefall only to end up hitting a rock? That's how my love life had turned out to be. And I didn't know how to save myself from the bottomless pit of agony.

I held Sheru and sat with him for a long time that afternoon after reaching home.

'I've made some *lauki* and *roti*, should I bring it now?' Maa asked.

Even my lunch was as miserable as my life that day. Somehow, I finished the plate and tried to work on Doggles. I was making a list of potential investors who had already invested in the pet care market and would be interested in expanding. But soon, I fell asleep. When I woke up, the sun had already set and my room was dark and gloomy.

As I switched on the light, my phone beeped.

'How are you holding up, *bhai*?' Saransh messaged.

I didn't feel like responding and going back to sleep.

'I am going to a party with the Blue Oak kids tonight. Do you want to come along? There will be a lot of pretty single girls there,' he sent another message.

'*Nahin, yaar*. I am quite occupied with work tonight. Plus, my father is at home. So won't be possible,' I told him and kept my phone away.

The phone pinged again. I tried to ignore it but finally read the text. Only three words. 'Just tell her.'

'What?' I replied.

'How you feel.' I blinked. Before I could respond, another text showed up. 'If you're so much in love, just tell her.'

I had to wait a few minutes before I could type, 'Don't be ridiculous' without adding in some choice angry emojis.

The phone pinged again. I put it on silent

mode. Sometimes, when Saransh got some stupid idea, the best thing to do was ignore him and hope it went away.

It was a difficult night for me. My mind was occupied with a lot of thoughts. A part of me had always wondered if Jigyaasu was gay as it was impossible to not fall in love with a girl like Radhika after spending so much time with her. Little did I know that it was Radhika whose sexuality was different.

23

'I'm doing no such thing,' I said, during the English class, sitting on the last bench with Saransh. I realised my volume had been higher than I had intended and the teacher stopped to look who it was.

'If you won't, I will tell her,' Saransh said. Unlike what I'd hoped, he didn't stop pestering me about telling Radhika how I felt. Even worse, now that we were at school, he had switched from copy-paste texts like *tell her tell her* to muttering in my ear. He was an idiot who knew nothing about matters of the heart.

'Fine, imagine I tell her,' I said, trying to sound reasonable. 'What happens next?'

'You'll have a great load off your chest.'

'And if we ever manage to stay friends after that it'll always be awkward between us. I'm not going to sabotage my friendship like that.'

'You still care about her that much?'

I couldn't respond right away. Did I care about her that much? Of course, I did. Why wouldn't I? Just because caring about her was making me die a thousand deaths every single day, doesn't mean I would stop.

'Attention class,' Ritu Ma'am announced. 'There is a poetry summit being organised in our school next week. So, if any of you want to participate, let me know.'

Jigyaasu and Neha Sitharam raised their arms immediately. But my eyes looked for Radhika, who was also looking at me. She knew that I would urge her to participate, but she was already shaking her head. I turned to her, but she shook her head so violently that even Jigyaasu looked at her in surprise.

'Anyone else? This is a unique opportunity, we'll probably invite some big poets over to judge the entries. You could really improve your talents and get some good contacts to help you in the business.'

She called out some names of students, some of whom grudgingly agreed. I could see Radhika's hands tugging at her tie, but she still did not meet my gaze.

'Radhika?' ma'am said.

She jumped like she was awaiting a scolding. 'Yes, ma'am?'

'Would you like to put your name in?'

Radhika looked at me in anger. Ritu ma'am had just called on her randomly, as she was sitting near the front and staring at the teacher. But I knew she thought I had requested the teacher to ask her. 'No, ma'am.'

Ritu Ma'am looked at me, perhaps understanding that I had suggested the whole poetry competition on her behalf. I badly wanted to lean over and convince her more earnestly, but I had to stay true to my promise not to force her.

I walked up to her the moment the class got over. 'Do you want me to give your name on your behalf?' I said. I realised I was using the same trick Saransh was trying to use on me just a few minutes back. But mine was for a better cause.

'You will do no such thing.' She gave me a blank look. 'My anxiety has been through the roof.'

She looked that way as well. Her tie was hanging an inch below her neck and she was twisting at her collar even now. I knew that it was not easy for her to say that. But brushing this conversation aside was not going to help us either. 'Sad that the world will miss out on hearing your lines,' I said, trying to keep my nudge as subtle as possible. But perhaps, I wasn't gentle enough because she whirled on me with such anger that I took a step back.

'Why don't you let me be, Yogesh? The world is not missing out on anything. It's not like I'm the greatest poet to have ever walked the planet or anything.'

I backed off. 'I'm sorry. I didn't mean to push you.'

'You have no idea what anxiety feels like, Yogesh.'

'Why don't you tell me?' I asked.

For a moment, she seemed honestly surprised that I asked her, and then thoughtful. 'It takes me forever to fall asleep. I think about every social situation I've been in, all the things I said or didn't say, till it drives me insane. I get antsy and nervous for even the littlest tasks. When everyone's eyes are on me, it feels like I will die,' she said.

'But you are going to die. What anxiety is telling is the truth. We are all going to die.'

'Like imagine if you had a friend who was constantly pointing out what is wrong with you and all the stupid things you have done in life. But you can't get rid of this friend because it is you. How do you get rid of yourself? I wish I knew what it's like to be normal. I keep feeling like the odd one out.'

'Well at this point,' I said, 'One in four people in the US have anxiety issues. So, there are a lot of people going through what you're going through.'

'Yes, but I can't console myself by telling myself that there are other people also going through what I'm going through. I am all I have got.'

'You know what is the trick to doing anything well?'

'What?' she asked.

'To do it badly.'

'What?'

'Yes, the trick to doing anything well is to do it badly.'

'Well, I'm great at doing things badly.'

'But anything worth doing is worth doing badly the first time. Our expectations paralyse us, and we cannot start anything new because we're afraid we'd flunk it up. 'You meant my desire to do something just right is holding me back.'

'Exactly. But just imagine, doing badly can free you up. Just start something, even a tiny step, without worrying about being good or bad. After a while, when you look back, you will realise you have come some way already and you were improving the entire time,' I smiled.

'I thought I knew the peak of my anxiety, but this is something else. I feel paralyzed,' she said. 'I feel like my feet are frozen.'

'In that case, let's go have some juice?' I asked. Radhika looked up immediately. She was expecting that I would give a pep talk or motivate her to go. 'That would be really nice,' she said.

'Why didn't you try to talk me into attending the poetry summit?' she asked, sipping on her watermelon juice.

'The thing about anxiety is that it makes everything feel bigger than it actually is. Look at it this way instead: it doesn't matter whether you go or not. Nobody is going to realise whether you're there or not. Even if you were the best poet in the world, they have no idea whether you're good or bad.'

'And why should I worry when they're not going to pay much attention to me anyway?' She smiled, and immediately seemed calmer, a clear sign that her anxiety was receding. She got up and started walking back towards the school. I followed her without asking any questions.

Ritu Ma'am was just winding up for the day in the staff room. Radhika went up to her and mumbled a few words. I was standing next to her, as Ritu Ma'am looked on.

'Really? Do you have something ready?' the teacher asked, after Radhika repeated herself.

Radhika blanked on hearing that. On one hand, she had tens of poems ready. On the other hand, she wasn't ready to share any of those with the teacher. I nudged her and smiled, but I didn't speak. I had promised her I would not push her into doing anything she was uncomfortable with. So I waited for her to make her choice.

And then, she nodded.

'Can you read it to me right now?' the teacher asked.

'Here?' Radhika asked. She looked around. I could tell that the presence of other teachers and the commotion in the room were intimidating for her.

'If you don't mind,' the teacher said.

I hoped with all my heart that she would say yes.

'Okay,' Radhika said and looked for something in her bag. It was her diary. She took it out and stared at it blankly as if she was illiterate. And then, I heard her whisper, 'Do it badly,' to herself. Standing there in the staff room, as teachers of varying levels of busyness packed their bags to leave, Radhika read the most beautiful poem I had ever heard.

I felt exhilarated as I came out of the staff room. By the time Radhika finished, every teacher in the room stopped doing what they were doing and listened to her. When she ended, each one of them clapped. And I clapped harder than all of them. If I felt so overwhelmed with my emotions, I could only imagine what she was feeling. I was proud, happy and clearly, still *madly in love*.

'That was amazingggg, Radhika,' I said and hugged her. A part of me ached from the previous day's heartbreaking revelation. But I wasn't going to let that take away from the moment of celebration.

'I wouldn't have been able to do this without you,' she smiled and hugged me back.

All my feelings for her that I had tried so hard to rid myself of in the last few days, returned in a jiffy. Truth be told, they had always been there. And seeing her acing her performance on stage that day made me feel even strongly towards her somehow.

'No, this is your victory. I am so proud of you. How did you do that?' I asked.

'Should I tell you the truth or should I make up a better answer?' she replied.

'I definitely want to know the truth as whatever you did clearly worked.'

She looked more serious all of a sudden. 'Well, to be honest, my mother had told me the same 5-4-3-2-1 method that you did, but I didn't listen to her then. But when ma'am asked me if I wanted to read something to her, it helped me in diverting my mind from the actual reading till the final moment.'

From the look on her face, I knew she did not want me to discuss her mother at the moment.

'Sometimes,' she continued, 'the simplest things have the greatest impact. Plus, when I was finally reading, I just ignored the voices in my head and went for it. I thought there's no harm in being bad at something, after all,' she smiled.

'Guess I've been a great life coach then,' I said.

'And a greater friend,' she added.

'Friend... yes.'

24

'Isn't that adorable? Even the photographer said it came out better than he expected.'

Radhika had printed out one of the pictures from the studio so we could look at it together; the rest were on her phone. Now that the editing and finishing touches were done, it was time to upload them on our site. She had captured a moment of Sheru mid-leap, as he ran through the lawn. The focus was nearly perfect, as we could see the details of the Doggles, and his hanging tongue. Sheru clearly looked delighted. Even as I looked at the picture, I remembered how truly blessed I was to have dogs, the most beautiful creatures, in my life. They asked for so little and gave so much.

'This one is definitely a keeper,' I said. 'I wish I could frame it. But my dad would break the frame and make a bonfire out of the wood on Lohri.'

'I'll frame it and keep it in my room,' she said, putting it away. 'I'm so excited to see how the pictures will look on the site.'

'It should be ready in a week.'

'And the process will begin for you to become the youngest billionaire ever.'

'Youngest-self-made-billionaire,' I added.

'You're BACK,' screamed my father as I entered the house. Sheru was barking in the background. He was as startled as I was.

I nervously entered the living room and noticed the whiskey glass on the table. I also realised that Maa was not home. Maybe she had gone to buy some groceries. I was alone at home with my drunk father and for some reason, he looked angrier than ever. His eyes were slightly red and I had never felt this scared of him before.

'What have you been UP TO?' he asked in an unnaturally high voice.

'What do you mean?' I asked and just then, my eyes fell on the sleek black top of my laptop on the sofa next to him. 'How did you get so MUCH MONEY?' he asked.

Shit. I wondered how he found it. I would always keep it in my shelf and I was sure I hadn't taken it out recently. 'Did you go through my things?'

'This is my house, I can go through whatever I want.' Before I could say anything, he shouted again, 'Tell me what have you been up to. Are you involved in some fishy *dhanda*? Have you been betting or something? Tell me.'

I felt disgusted that my dad thought so lowly of me. Like always, I wanted to walk away and not entertain his insults. But I knew things could take an ugly turn if I didn't speak then.

'How do you think I've been paying for my expenses? I have been working. This is my hard-earned money. And no, I don't participate in any shady *dhanda wanda*,' I snapped.

'Then how do you explain having such a large amount? I thought you'd been taking care of your regular expenses with tuition money or maybe a small job at a cyber cafe.'

'I don't give tuition anymore. I don't work at a cyber cafe either.'

'Then what the hell do you do?' he demanded.

'I work as a dog walker.'

'*Hain*? What?'

'I have a clientele of dog owners in a posh society near Fountain Park. I take their dogs for walks every morning and sometimes, in the evenings too. I make about 8-9 thousand every month.'

For a microsecond, he looked like he was relieved to know that his son was not a drug peddler or gambler. But soon, that relief was replaced with even more anger than before.

'You got a stray dog at our house. I said nothing. You decided to keep him for good. I said nothing. You are developing a stupid business idea of dog glasses. I said nothing. But working like a servant to earn some money from the rich families of Faridabad? Do you also clean dog shit for some extra tips?'

'What? It is a respectable job. Dog walking is a common profession in the western countries,' I tried to make a case for myself.

'But we are not from those countries. If someone from our area spots you walking the dogs of some elites just for a few bucks? You know how insulting that will be?'

'I am making my own money with my hard work and I am not even eighteen yet. This should make you feel proud and not insulted,' I shouted back.

'Your obsession with dogs and making money is getting out of hand. School se ghar, ghar se school. You are not allowed to go anywhere else from today,' he ordered.

'But why? While other guys -'

I was cut mid-sentence as my father threw his whisky glass in my direction. He probably deliberately missed me, but I was shaken by the sound of the steel striking the floor. I didn't know how to react or what to say to him. I noticed that I was shaking. I felt in danger like I had never before. I believed it was just best to leave the house until he calmed down.

I didn't have anywhere to go. I ran like my

life depended on it. Running so fast had a numbing effect on me. I felt my anger subsiding gradually. My mind felt like a thoughtless abyss. I kept running for a while. After a long time, when I felt a cramp on my left calf, I slowed down a little. The vicinity I was in looked strangely familiar. Then I realised where I was. I was two lanes away from Narendra Library. I checked the time on my phone. It was almost 9 pm. Another hour before the shop would shut for the day. So,I decided to visit Narru Uncle. I also wanted to catch my breath and drink some water, to be honest. Plus, I wanted to stay away from home and *that man* for as long as I could that night.

'You look pale, *beta*,' Nauru Uncle said as soon as he spotted me inside the shop.

I asked for some water and guzzled it down before getting into some generic small talk with him. After a couple of minutes, I walked towards the non-fiction shelf. I picked up the biography of Steve Jobs. I had read somewhere that the book was on Elon Musk's reading list as well.

'Yogesh,' I heard a familiar voice say.

Wearing a green shirt with khaki shorts,

Radhika looked like she was ready for a jungle safari. She pulled off her offbeat outfit choice for a library visit really well. And seeing her gave me a strange sense of calm after the storm I had weathered. I sat down on the stool next to her.

'Listen, you two are going to be here for a while, right? I have to run a quick errand. Can you please take care of the store till I return?' Narendra Uncle asked us.

'Sure, uncle,' we said in unison.

'Are you okay?' she asked.

'The usual. My dad being his usual… self.' I shrugged my shoulders and it was as if that was enough for her to know every single detail of what had happened with my father. She not only knew by that shrug that I had fought with him but also that the intensity of this fight was higher than the usual ones. It was almost as if she knew every single sentence I had exchanged with him.

'I'm so sorry this happened,' she said with empathetic eyes.

'I know you've been through worse. But maybe I'm not as brave as you,' I blurted out in response. Just then my eyes fell on her cheeks. Through the dim lighting of the library, I saw trails of dry tears on her cheeks. I had been so lost in my own pain that I didn't realise that she was going through something as well.

'What happened?' I said, pointing at her dry tears.

She just looked down without answering. It was my turn to understand her silence. It was about her mother. It was as if the two of us had a whole non-verbal vocabulary. We knew each other too well by now.

'Did she call again?' I asked.

Radhika was looking down, but she nodded.

'Did you pick it?' I asked.

'Yes,' she said.

'And?'

'She wants to meet me,' Radhika said, the end of her sentence almost trailing off. I just stood there looking at her. She stepped forward and lifted her arms. I realised that she was hugging me. I realised at that moment that I had never hugged a girl my age. I held her and my fingertips had never touched a back as soft as hers'. My nose had smelled girls' shampoo, but never from this close. My cheeks touched her ears and I felt something move deep inside me. I wanted to let myself flow. It was the first time I was feeling something I had only read in books and seen in movies.

She reached out for my hand and gripped it softly and said, 'The good news is that we are not our parents. We are carving our own path and making our own identity. We are too full of kindness to abandon anyone, least of all our own flesh and blood. I feel so lucky to have met you, Yogesh. The most important thing is that you care. And you care about the right things. You should be -'

'Radhika,' I interrupted her as I broke the hug and looked deep into her eyes.

'Yes?'

'I'm madly in love with you,' I heard myself say. It was almost as if I had no control over the words coming out of my mouth.

END OF PART 1

WHAT LIES AHEAD

So, Yogesh's long-held secret has finally come to light.

But how will Radhika respond to this unexpected revelation?

Continue this beloved story of Yogesh and Radhika in the sequel to this book, this time from Radhika's perspective.

The story continues where Extra Class has left off, exploring more of Radhika's life.

An artist's life is a challenging one, and anxiety always makes it worse. Explore how Radhika navigates her passions and battles her inner demons.

You will also find out more about Radhika's complex relationship with her mother and her girlfriend Gagan.

And of course, you will get more of your favourite duo as they manouevre around this event in their relationship.

Book 2 in the 'Extra Class' series releasing on 1st July 2024

ABOUT THE AUTHOR

'Extra Class: The First Crush,' written by Sachin Garg under the pen name Sidharth Oberoi. Sachin is a bestselling author, popular speaker and serial entrepreneur based out of Mumbai. He has written articles for Huffington Post and Scroll.in and has been featured in most leading newspapers and magazines. He has also spoken at numerous Indian and International forums like South Asia Media Summit (Islamabad), TEDx (Allahabad) and several IITs and IIMs.

Email: me.sachingarg@gmail.com

Instagram: @gargsachin